CW00864589

ALWAYS
AND
FOREVER

CAROL
PROBYN

This novel begins and ends in the
village of Claines, Worcestershire where my
grandmother lived and told me stories of the
school and church.
The church, school, rectory and the
Mug Inn are still standing today.
The Grange is imaginary, but based
on an existing house.
The rural setting depicted hasn`t
changed dramatically except of course for
the obvious modern housing along
Cornmeadow Lane and the motorway link
beneath School Bank.

Most of the story is set against the
background of the First World War, and I
have tried to be as accurate as possible
regarding the battles and main events.
However, all characters and events
other those than clearly in the public
domain are fictitious, and any resemblance
to real persons, living or dead, is purely co-
incidental.

Acknowledgements

*Much of my research was
conducted via the Internet. Sites that were
particularly useful were;
B.B,C, Channel 4
The National Archives
FANY – Our Proud History
The Long, Long Trail
Imperial War Museum
WW1 Document Archive*

*My grateful thanks to patient
friends who have proof-read and given
positive feed-back on this book.
To dear Sue (her final favour to
me), Dorothy, Lucy, my Writing Group,
and last but not least Jo Mayo, without
whose help with self-publication, this novel
would never have seen the light of day.*

This book is dedicated to the memory of Grandad Jack Digger who cared for many of the war horses in his regiment.

Like so many of the Tommies who survived, he spoke little of his experiences. Now that I have researched so much about that dreadful war I understand why

One

"Lyddy her you are!"

Lydia scuffed to a halt on the old swing, pulled her skirt down and leapt forward to embrace her brother.

"Alfred! About time too!"

She squeezed her eyes shut, laughing in delight as their cheeks touched. When she opened them, she looked over Alfred`s shoulder, and the handsomest boy she had ever seen was smiling back at her. Oh heavens! Seconds ago she had been swinging high, legs in the air like a ten year old! What if…

"Lyddy!" Alfred grabbed her hands and swung her round. "Look at you, so pretty in your ribbons and rosebuds!"

Lydia patted her hair and straightened her ribbons, aware that she was blushing, for although she was overjoyed to see her darling brother, she was very much aware of his friend with his crooked smile and dark, appraising eyes.

"This is Jack Albright, my friend from college. Jack meet my little sister Lydia."

Jack took her hand and shook it gently. His hands were soft and cool, softer than hers. "Miss Winters. Very pleased to meet you."

For once in her life Lydia was speechless, and it wasn`t just that she was unaccustomed to being addressed like a grown-up – like a lady. He literally took her breath away, with his soft touch and his dark, dancing eyes.

Alfred coughed. "Come on Lyddy. Look, Polly has poured lemonade for us. Ma and Pa are waiting."

Her brother took her arm and led her down the

garden path towards the table under the horse-chestnut tree. She straightened her back and summoned up as much dignity as she could, hoping Jack wouldn`t notice that her dress was too short. Why did she care? But she did. Oh, what must he think of me in this silly pink rosebud dress which makes me look like a child! But then her father thought she still was a child. Father! She could see him waiting for them at the bottom of the path, and he was sure to notice her scuffed boots.

"There you are, madam!" Sure enough her father glared at her boots as Jack held out one of the old metal chairs for her to sit. "I know Alfred was late, but you could have waited patiently with your mother and me."

"Yes, Father." Lydia folded her hands in her lap and dropped her eyes.

"Never mind, Henry, all`s well." Eliza, Lydia`s mother smiled at her husband. Alfred immediately broke the tension by talking about Oxford, where he had just completed his second year studying law. It was the beginning of the summer holidays and the family had been awaiting his arrival with great excitement.

Polly, their maid of all work, served seed cake and lemonade, and as she leant over Lydia whispered, "There`s a split under your arm. I`d keep very still if I was you."

"Thank you, Polly," Lydia murmured, the blood rushing in her ears.

She nibbled at the cake which her mother had baked specially, hoping it would be good enough for Alfred`s friend, Jack Albright, son of a solicitor from

Leamington Spa and Member of Parliament, the Honourable Francis Albright.

She stole a glance at Jack, marvelling at this handsome young man with his broad shoulders, curly dark hair and cultured voice. And oh, that smile! She looked away, not trusting herself to meet those deep, dark eyes.

"…and congratulations to you Lydia for passing the King`s Scholarship." Alfred was raising his glass of lemonade.

"Well done Miss Lydia," smiled Jack joining the toast. "This makes you a fully qualified teacher, I presume?"

Lydia nodded, her mouth full of cake. Her father glared.

"I do so respect anyone who teaches. Lydia - and you too of course Mr. Winters – you both have my full admiration."

Thankfully her father left soon afterwards leaving the boys to unpack, and Lydia was glad to escape to her room, where she couldn`t wait to rid herself of her dress. She put on her every-day striped blouse and flung open her window for air. Now she was rid of that tight bodice with a hole under the arm (oh, the shame!), she felt able to breathe again. But it wasn`t just the dress. It was a hot summer day, but even so, she felt as if her face had been flushed and her breathing out of control ever since she had laid eyes on Jack Albright. She splashed some tepid water from her washstand onto her face, and frowned into the mirror. Thankfully the ringlets that Polly had curled so carefully earlier in the day were losing their

3

shape, but oh, those silly ribbons! Still, she had better keep them in to please her mother.

She went to the window again, and looked up the garden to the elderberry bushes, beyond which she could just see the top of the old swing. She had waited there for Alfred because it was their special place; where they had played as children and where more recently they went to talk out of earshot of the parents. It was where Alfred had sobbed when he had returned home, aged thirteen, after his first term at boarding school because he had been so unhappy. The older boys had laughed at the schoolmaster`s boy and had bullied him. Lydia had been outraged, but he had sworn her to secrecy. "It`s just the way it is, I`m not the only one." He said it had got easier for him, but Lydia had always doubted it. Father would slap him on the back and say it was making a man of him, but young as she was, Lydia sensed it came at a price for her clever, sensitive brother. Nevertheless, he was now at his second year at Oxford studying law. Things must be better for him there, for here he was, friends with a Member of Parliament`s son.

She heard the boys laughing, still sitting at the table under the tree. Yes, the difference in Alfred this time was obvious. She had never seen him so at ease, so confident, and it must have something to do with Jack.

"Lyddy!" Alfred called, seeing her at the window. "We`re going for a stroll over to Bevere, fancy coming?"

Lydia waved and quickly pulled on her navy-blue skirt. She was now dressed in her teacher`s `uniform`, but she felt more at ease. Now that she was earning a modest wage she would buy a new summer dress, one that fitted.

The boys were in the hall. "Come on slow-coach," laughed Alfred.

Lydia could hardly contain herself. "I`ll just get my hat."

"I think not Lydia. Polly will need help in the kitchen," her father said from the doorway.

Jack caught her eye and gave her a sympathetic look.

Alfred tucked her under the chin. "Cheer up. Here, this is for you. A belated eighteenth birthday present."

She had received a birthday card from him the month before, and now she took the parcel and carefully unwrapped the brown paper covering. It was a beautifully bound, blue leather notebook. "It`s lovely Alfred, thank you."

"I thought you could write a diary or something. Or maybe write out your favourite poems."

Lydia hugged the book to her chest and nodded.

"We're here for a week Miss Winters. Hopefully you can join us some other time," Jack smiled.

"Please call me Lydia."

"Lydia." The way he said it, it was as if she had never heard her name before.

She watched through the hall window as they walked down the front path – her short, stocky brother, his straight hair combed and parted meticulously, and tall, graceful Jack, his dark, curly hair a bit longer than was usually seen, for it grew over his collar. There was a slight touch of arrogance about him, which even the unsophisticated Lydia recognised. But oh, when he had smiled, it had made her heart miss a beat.

She ran upstairs, placed the book on her dressing table and took a folded note from her drawer. Earlier that day she had helped Polly drag her iron bed into Alfred`s room for their visitor to sleep in, and had made up the bed. Now, she crept in and slipped the paper under Alfred`s pillow. It was a short poem she had copied out earlier, and she had glued a tiny pressed buttercup at the bottom. She hesitated, as it suddenly occurred to her that her brother might now belittle this ritual. After all, he was now an undergraduate, mixing with the sons of the gentry, as her father never tired of reminding everyone. Well, let it be the last time, like it was the last time she wore a little girl`s dress.

Later, at dinner, between mouthfuls of steak and kidney pie, Eliza asked Jack about his family.

"I am the eldest of three, Mrs. Winters. I have a brother of fifteen and a sister of ten. My brother is at Rugby and little Theresa is tutored at a day school at the moment. I shall be going home to see them after our walking holiday."

"Goodness! We have the pleasure of your company before your own family," Eliza exclaimed.

"Yes, well father will be in Westminster until then, and Thomas at school. Mother thought it better that they would all be there to greet me."

"I do hope you don`t find us too quiet and quaint in this little Worcestershire backwater, Jack."

Henry coughed and gave his wife a warning glare.

"No, indeed. I find myself quite at home already."

"And when do you plan to embark on your walking tour – Cumberland is it not?"

"Next Saturday, Father. We need to go into town and get kitted out first."

"Perhaps you gentlemen would care to join me in the parlour for a glass of port wine?" Henry said at the end of the meal, leaving Polly and Lydia to wash the dishes.

*

"We all used to stay together after supper, ma," Lydia said when she sat with her mother in the kitchen.

"Yes, I know dear. But I suppose your father realises that Alfred is a young man now, and in Jack's circles the gentlemen retire to drink port or brandy, smoke and talk about serious things."

Lydia wrinkled her nose. "Well they can keep the smoking and drinking, but can't we talk about serious things?"

"Of course, darling, but the fact is that the men run the world, even though they make a mess of it most of the time. Then we have to put it all back together again."

Lydia smiled at her mother's gentle wisdom. Everything is changing, she thought to herself. Alfred was older and he would no longer have time for her like he used to. She had seen subtle changes in his demeanour the last time he was home, and seeing him with Jack it was obvious how he looked up to him. He was so much more confident and appeared a little more distant from her. It was obvious he was trying to model himself on Jack, and at times he seemed a little stiff and pompous.

The door and windows were open as the weather had been humid, but Lydia suddenly felt as constricted as she had in her rosebud dress. She had never thought too much about her future, but suddenly the thought of endless days of rote-teaching compact rows of little children and sitting here every night with her mother, filled her with apprehension. On the other hand, Alfred was becoming a man – he was now twenty, and he had so many choices open to him. For the first time in her life she felt envious. She banished the thought instantly. She was an educated young lady who should be grateful for her station in life. This was a favourite phrase of her father's. Stations in life! She sighed and looked at her dear mother. How she must have loved Henry, her father, for Lydia knew that her family had disowned her when she had married him. She was in her late forties, and still a fine looking woman. Her dark hair, streaked a little with grey was drawn back into a bun, the simple style she always wore. Lydia had inherited her high cheekbones, but not her light brown eyes and slightly aquiline nose. Apparently Lydia resembled her mother's mother, whom she had never known. She wondered if her mother ever regretted giving up a more privileged life, especially now as she toiled into the evening, mending her husband's socks. For the first time Lydia wondered if her mother was happy with her station in life.

Two

Alfred had a silly grin on his face, and Jack looked a little flushed when they came into the kitchen later. Evidence indeed, of drinking port wine, thought Lydia. He held out his hand. "Come on Lydia. We're just going to take a turn down the lane before bed. It's a beautiful, light June evening. Let's make the best of it."Lydia's heart sang, but as she got up from the table, she looked at her mother for approval, as her father was nowhere to be seen.

"Go on. I'm sure your father won't mind now. But don't be too long."

Hatless and carefree, Lydia took Alfred's arm, and was thrilled to be holding onto her brother once more. Then to her surprise, Jack took her other arm, and threaded it through his. She felt as light as air, and as if it was the most natural thing in the world to be walking down the hill between the two most wonderful boys in creation.

School House, its garden and school building sat in an elevated position surrounded by meadows and fields. The back garden eventually met the rear grounds of the rectory to the one side, and rolling fields to the other. In front, the narrow lane led to the right down towards the lovely old Norman Church of St. John with its square tower. They passed Claines Institute on the way, venue for many a social gathering and where Lydia attended choir practice. It also housed the small Post Office, which operated out of the living room at the back. Charlie Tombs, caretaker and sexton to the church lived there with his family. Mary, his wife who ran the post office waved to them as they passed.

They paused a little further to look at the lovely old Church, which dominated the area at the crossroads. The higgledy-piggledy headstones in the graveyard cast long shadows in the late June evening.

They crossed over to Cornmeadow Lane. "And that, dear Jack," said Alfred "is the famous Mug Inn. The only public house in England built on consecrated ground."

Jack expressed his surprise. "A pub in a churchyard! I'll wager many a member of the congregation has been glad of a glass of ale after a lengthy service, eh?"

Church Manor House, the impressive Regency house of a glove-making factory owner in Worcester was opposite. A few small cottages edged the lane, and some of the men were working on their vegetable patches, and wives and children sat languidly on doorsteps. They all knew the Winters, and waved or called out greetings to them as they passed. Orchards and barley fields stretched away into the distance beyond, and ox-eye daisies and a few buttercups and clover jostled for company with straggly poppies in the long grass edging the road.

Lydia eagerly asked questions about Oxford, and Jack waxed lyrical about the city of dreaming spires, and the beauty of Magdalene. "It sits amid a hundred acres of woodland, riverside walks and even has its own deer park."

Lydia listened with rapt attention as he described Addison`s Walk and the great meadow with its stunning display of snakehead fritillaries in April. Alfred had told her about the college but in more prosaic terms.

They paused at a stile leading to a field of barley. Lydia watched as he deftly climbed over and carried on walking along the path at the side of the field, pausing only to pick an ear of barley. The sun was low in the pink sky with wisps of angel-hair clouds; not a breath of air stirred the crops. Jack quickly clambered over and helped her down.

"Shall we go as far as the river, Lydia?" Alfred asked.

"Oh, it`s so hot, and I think it`s a little late, Alfred."

The Thames when it gets to Oxford becomes the Isis," said Jack dreamily.

"How romantic!" said Lydia.

The expression on Jack`s face when he turned towards her made Lydia catch her breath. He turned away, and pushed Alfred forward playfully. "And then there`s the Cherwell. On May Day morning students jump into it from the Magdalene Bridge."

Alfred snorted. "Some students do!"

Jack threw his head back and laughed. Lydia could picture it – Jack and other madcap students splashing about in the river, whilst Alfred watched, probably too afraid of getting his suit ruined. Dear boy!

"We have been punting haven`t we Alfred?" Jack tore at a few poppy heads at the edge of the field.

"We have indeed! You must come Lydia, we'll punt you along the Cherwell!"

"Can I, can I really come and visit, Alfred?" Lydia could think of nothing she would like more.

"Why yes, of course you silly girl. Of course you shall come."

"You shall wear a dress of white muslin, and you shall float along the river like the Lady of Shalott" laughed Jack.

Lydia was thrilled. "Do you like Tennyson?"

"He is a great favourite of mine." smiled Jack, then he suddenly stopped.

"But stand still!" He reached out and loosened her ribbons, as Lydia stood motionless. He arranged her fine, light brown hair – still retaining the curls - to fall over each shoulder. He lifted her chin and stared into her blue eyes; cornflower blue in this light against her flawless, pale skin. For the second time that day the world stopped turning for Lydia. She lost herself in his fathomless dark eyes and she held her breath. Was he going to kiss her? But he just smiled his lop-sided smile and said huskily; "Oh, yes!"

Lydia was entranced, and blushed to the roots of her hair.

Alfred's voice broke the spell. "I say, Jack old chum!"

Lydia dropped her eyes and giggled self-consciously. Her cheeks were burning, her heart racing.

"But don't you see Alfred! The likeness is astonishing! Look, look at your sister, her hair, her eyes!"

Alfred frowned at his sister, who shrugged back at him.

"I might never have seen it – oh, I'm sure I would eventually – but I was reminded of the painting when we talked about the poem. Lydia so resembles the Lady of Shalott!"

"Does she?"

"Do I?" Brother and sister frowned at each other.

"Forgive me. Perhaps you have never seen it. It was painted by…by… John Waterman, Waterhouse… oh, something like that Anyway, it has become very famous indeed. I saw it in London, oh, at the Royal Academy? I'm not sure. Anyway, it made a tremendous impact on me."

Alfred coughed. "Fancy that Lydia, you look like the Lady of Shalott."

"Yes, yes, and it is a work of art you both must see!" Jack was still looking at Lydia in wonder.

But the moment of magic was slowly evaporating for Lydia, for didn't the Lady of the poem die? She took the proffered ribbons from Jack and re-tied her hair behind her, making a mental note to look up the poem at her earliest opportunity. The boys began re-tracing their steps and she instinctively hung back as they laughed and joked together.

"Now I remember another poem from the Old Laureate, much more to my liking." Alfred started reciting;

Half a league, half a league,
Half a league onward,
All in the valley of Death
Rode the six hundred!"

Jack joined in at the second verse, but although Lydia knew the words well for some reason she felt a sense of foreboding and exclusion. But she feigned a smile and clapped. "Bravo!"

Her brother gave a mock bow and hopped over the style, looking pleased with himself. Jack plucked a poppy and handed her the flower with a slight bow. She took the flower, but as it trembled in her hand, the fragile petals dropped away. Seeing her disappointment he plucked another.

"It should be a cornflower to match your eyes."

"Come on Lyddy!" called Alfred reaching for her hand as she climbed the stile. "I can remember the time when you would have jumped over here!" He grabbed her hand crushing the leaves of the poppy. It left a slight stain on the palm of her hand, and a little wave of sadness dispelled the enchantment, just for a second.

The three of them resumed their previous arrangement, but now Lydia was acutely conscious of Jack`s closeness, and savoured every moment. She sensed the slight changes in the tension of his muscles and studied the line of his jaw as he talked and turned to smile at her. She could smell the soap he used, and something else, a male scent that was different to anything she had sensed before, anywhere.

When they returned to School House it was dusk, and Lydia reluctantly let Jack release her. Eliza was still sitting at her sewing in the kitchen with the door ajar for coolness.

"Father has gone to his bed, and I`m just off. Come along now, Lydia."

She murmured "goodnight" and climbed the stairs in a daze. She lay on her bed, staring out at the stars for a long time, reliving the episode in the barley field over and over again.

*

In their bedroom, Jack threw himself down on Alfred's bed. Alfred was about to protest, but checked himself. It was only polite to give up his bed for his guest.

As Alfred was just about to blow out the candle, Jack stopped him.

"Hold on Alfred. There's something under my pillow." He sat up and opened the folded paper.

"Why, it's a poem and a buttercup!"

"Oh yes. It's a little ritual Lydia and I had, for a long time. We called them Pillow Poems." Alfred looked a little shame-faced as he explained. "It all started when Lydia was about eight. Father had given her a most awful thrashing for some silly behaviour – I think we had been to tea with the vicar. Poor thing cried her heart out all evening. I crept into her room when she was asleep that night and slipped a poem under her pillow to cheer her up. From then on, it became something we did from time to time. You know, to cheer each other up."

Jack was fascinated. "I've never heard anything so charming, that's marvellous. You are lucky having such a splendid sister."

"Yes, I am aren't I?" Alfred grinned. "Nowadays of course, she writes to me and always sends me a few verses. That one's to welcome me home I suppose. Let me see it." Alfred held out his hand.

"Wait, I'm not sure it's for you Perhaps Lydia has started a new tradition. After all it was under my pillow."

"I don't think so. You have my bed, I'm sleeping in Lydia's. She's made a mistake - thought you would be sleeping in this one."

"Well, where's Lydia sleeping then?" asked Jack incredulously.

"On the truckle bed, I suppose. It's what we do when we have guests. She doesn't mind a bit."

"Poor little Lydia!" said Jack

"Why poor little Lydia? She won't mind I assure you."

"Did your father used to thrash her much?"

"Eh? Well, no not much. He is very strict you know, and Lydia is so clumsy and reckless at times. I think father despairs that she will ever be a lady. Of course, I used to get a beating sometimes too."

Beatings were a fact of life, Jack thought. He had been beaten, usually by his mother, but somehow he couldn't bear the thought of Lydia being thrashed.

"I'm hardly a man of the world, but being a lady isn't everything. I like your sister. I think she's perfectly splendid." Oh, far, far more than that!

"Yes, so you said." Alfred sounded a little petulant.

"And I think I shall keep her poem." Jack closed his eyes and relived the scene in the barley field. How he had wanted to take her in his arms.

"Do as you like" said Alfred and blew out the candle.

16

Lydia eventually lit her own candle and found her volume of Poems by Tennyson containing The Lady of Shalott. She read it slowly, and immersed herself in the beauty of the poet's lyrical rhythm. But she had been right; it was a tragedy of epic proportions. She had been enthralled when Jack had compared her to a character in a poem, and said that she looked like a famous painting! But it was so sad, for the lady had died. Surely it could not be a bad omen? Of course not, all those poems based on myths and legends were tragic. This was 1914 – this was today!

She licked the stain on her palm, and hugged herself as she re-lived this extraordinary day - especially the moment in the barley field. She felt sure he would have kissed her if Alfred had not been there, and she most definitely would have let him, even though she hadn't been kissed since Freddie Maycroft had pecked her on the cheek over a year ago. Today she had felt something surge within her, a burning ripple through to her heart, to her throat, because it had stopped her from breathing. And she could have lost herself in his fathomless dark eyes forever.

There was much in the poem she still did not understand, however, but she now knew just what to write in her precious notebook. Something which would be worthy of that precious first page.

Three

Lydia sat in front of her speckled mirror and brushed her hair. She draped it over her shoulders, as Jack had done the night before. Jack! He said she looked like the Lady in a famous painting; a painting which had had an enormous impact on him. Dare she hope that she, little Lydia Winters had also made an enormous impact on him? She had read so many poems about love, had heard her friends talking about love, and had sung many a song about love. Is this what it felt like – to be `in love`? It had to be, for although she recognised the reflection in the mirror, she no longer felt the same inside. It seemed she had a heightened awareness of everything around her one minute – the texture of her own hair, the patina on the mirror, the sound of the birds outside, and the next minute she found it hard to concentrate on a single task, and her surroundings were a blur. And all the time, she kept seeing Jack – her head was full of Jack. She recalled that the poem had told of the Lady of Shalott weaving a magic web of images of the world that were reflected in the mirror. She would be cursed if she looked directly on the world. And of course, the arrival of the bold Sir Lancelot had caused her to do so, and she is doomed.

Lydia felt a slight shiver and looked over her shoulder. Surely there was no connection between the poem and her life. Poems were so often full of tragedy! Well her life would not be tragic, she felt determined.

She checked her top button on her blouse in the mirror, and blushed. She remembered the brief moment in the barley field when something overwhelming had passed between them. He said that she was beautiful. Yes, something momentous had happened, and Lydia would hold onto that precious something forever.

As she heard her mother descend the stairs, she resolved that whatever the day would bring, she must keep her feelings under control. It wasn't only her father and mother she would be letting down. She had sensed Alfred's discomfort in the barley field. But then, she was after all his little sister, not someone to be compared to a work of art! She pinched her cheeks and carried her chamber pot downstairs.

Her heart gave a little lurch when she met Jack's eyes at breakfast, and he smiled his gracious greetings to everyone. She nibbled at her bread and said little, relieved that everything seemed so normal.

"A breakfast fit for a king, Mrs.Winters!" Jack thanked Eliza, then followed Alfred out into the garden, nodding graciously to Lydia. This was the beginning of presenting a composed face to the world, while inwardly her heart beat furiously.
She went into the scullery to help Polly with the dishes.

"You works like a good 'un you do, 'specially draggin' your bed next door and helping' me make 'em up."

"It's no bother Polly. We couldn't have a gentleman sleeping on a truckle bed!"

"Ooh, and what a gentleman 'e is then! What an 'ansome young fellow he is, if you don't mind me sayin' so!"

19

Lydia giggled. "I quite agree Polly, he is very handsome indeed!"

"Mind you, Master Alfred be every bit as much the gentleman these days too. Not too grand to remember Polly though. He asked after me family too."

"Well of course Polly! He`s known you all his life."

"Yeah, I know Miss, but we was kids then. Our lives go in very different directions now, don`t they?"

Polly turned her sharp, freckled little face towards her, and her hard stare made Lydia feel a little uncomfortable, for she was right of course. Polly lifted a red, chapped hand out of the water and tucked a stray ginger hair into her old fashioned mop cap.

"I`ll just throw this water away, and I`ll be off. There`ll be plenty to do at `ome. I`ll pop in and see the Missus, and remind her to put the joint in. See you tomorrow Miss."

Lydia caught her hand gently as she was about to leave.

"Polly, I know things are changing, but I hope we`ll always be friends."

Polly gave a wry smile. "Course we will, Miss Lydia, but in a few years, likely it`ll be you as`ll be Mistress of this school, and I`ll still be scrubbin` yer floors! `Bye for now Miss."

Another reminder of how things were changing. Polly was one of eight children and had left school at thirteen to work at School House, many left even earlier if they were needed on the land. Like most families round about, her money was desperately needed. Her father worked on the land for Squire Bengeworth, as did her older brothers and sister. Polly counted herself lucky though, as most girls in service left home and lived in. Polly received similar wages, and left when the chores were done, and had Saturday and Sunday afternoons free.

Although the same age, Polly was so worldly-wise compared to Lydia. When Freddie Maycroft had kissed her at the Christmas dance, she asked Polly if she would have a baby. Polly had laughed until she cried, and explained in lurid detail just how babies were made, leaving Lydia horrified at the prospect of intimate contact with the opposite sex. She thought it was amazing that at least three girls she went to school with were now married with babies.

"Lydia, dreaming again! You`ll be late for Sunday School." Her mother`s voice reminded her of her present duties.

She made her way to the schoolroom where she took a small class for Sunday School. Afterwards most parents collected their children for the main church service, and the rest Lydia marched down the hill to St. John`s Church.

It was a fine, fresh summer morning, and as usual the lanes were busy with people making their way to church, most of them walking, but some on bicycles or packed into gigs and carts. Clutching her bible and with her neat little navy blue hat perched on her head, she checked the children were in line.

"Georgie Amphlett, stop jumping up and down. Sally Smith, hold his hand!" She led the children down the lane, passing Jack and Alfred at the cottage gate. Jack winked at her as she passed, and she heard Sally giggle.

Calls of "`Morning Miss Lydia!" resounded as people greeted her, and she smiled and nodded back, happy as a lark on this fine Sunday morning. Soon the church was packed, with all and sundry kitted out in their Sunday best. Lydia took her place, admiring the many large flower-decked hats in evidence. Inspired by the glorious day, the ladies were determined to give their best hats an airing. She smiled proudly as the children belted out the words she had taught them to "All things Bright and Beautiful".

She could see Jack seated with her family at right angles to her and the main congregation, in the pews reserved for gentry and respected of the parish. Behind them sat the Waltons and Morrises, two of the wealthiest farmers, and she could see her father and mother exchanging a few words with Dr. Morton and his wife, sitting beside them. The local Squire, Sir Frederick Bengeworth and his family, were sitting in their allocated seats opposite, as they always did. The Squire and his eldest son Edwin seemed to be taking particular interest in Jack.

After the service, she waited as Reverend Peabody introduced the local dignitaries to Jack, including the Squire and his family, and watched her parents glow with pride. The Bengeworths then swept past her, ignoring her as usual, in spite of the fact that the two youngest girls had spent a year at the school. Edwin, tall and elegant with finely chiselled features was last in the group, and he paused to lift his hat.

"Miss Lydia." He arched one eyebrow and appraised her from top to toe. It was the first time Lydia could remember him addressing her directly. He was gentry, and until today she had hardly raised her eyes to appraise him. But now his open stare made her blush and drop her eyes. She was relieved when he followed his family, who were climbing into their open carriage, waiting at the lychgate. Edwin climbed in to join them, looking every inch the Lord of the Manor he was destined to be.

A tug at her dress brought her back to earth. "Oh, dear, little Georgie Amphlett seems to have been abandoned yet again," Lydia lamented as her family joined her. Georgie did not seem to be bothered in the least as he held tightly onto her with one hand, and wiped his nose with the other. She forestalled her father's criticism of Georgie's parents him by offering to take him home

She heard her father's loud sigh as she whisked Georgie down the path, then Jack's voice. "Come along young fellow, we'll soon have you home for your family roast."

Henry looked surprised, glaring over his pince-nez, as Jack whisked the tiny boy, all skin and bone, and small for his five years, easily onto his shoulders and strode on in front of Lydia. How little he knows of such families, she thought to herself. The Amphletts will be lucky to be having bread and dripping for lunch.

Lydia and Jack had only just rounded the bend in the lane, when one of Georgie's older sisters came running towards them.

"Oooh, I'm sorry Miss Winters! You didn't 'ave to bring 'im. Mam says he can run 'ome, like 'e ran up!"

"Now, Sarah someone should bring him. Why don't you come yourself and attend church, or perhaps just Sunday School. Georgie was a bit fidgety in church."

"Well I would Miss, but since Mam has taken poorly with the babby, I 'as to 'elp and that."

Jack had swung the delighted Georgie to the ground and Sarah wiped his nose with the handkerchief Lydia proffered. Just then the clatter of hooves made them look up and Freddie Maycroft drew alongside driving his cart, with his mother Aggie sitting at his side. Seated in the back were the four of the Ganderton family - neighbours of theirs – all returning from morning service.

"Morning Miss Lydia," he smiled as he raised his cap, and the greeting was chorused by the Gandertons and their two children, but Aggie Maycroft stared grimly ahead.

"See you at choir practice, Freddie!" called Lydia as the cart passed them.

Georgie had skipped on down the lane, following his sister.

"Another admirer of yours?" asked Jack taking off his hat and examining it. Looking for dribbles no doubt, thought Lydia.

"Who? Georgie or Freddie?" she smiled, as they turned back up the lane.

"Why, Freddie of course, although, I shouldn`t be surprised if half the young eligible men in the parish weren`t in awe of you. Certainly you turned heads in church, and you even took the eye of the Squire`s son." Jack replaced his hat, and offered her his arm. She stopped.

"You are teasing me, Jack!"

"What? No, I`m not teasing, Lydia. You are quite a beauty, and I am by no means the only one to think that!"

"Don`t be foolish!" Lydia blushed and hurried on, ignoring his arm. He caught her up.

"I don`t wish to embarrass you, Lydia, but surely you must be aware that you are fine looking young lady."

"Well, I know I`m not ugly, and I`m thankful for that."

"No, indeed. Well, I can see you`re not used to compliments, and I can`t think why. Modest little Lydia."

"You do like giving me titles, Master Jack. Last night it was Lady Lydia, today it`s Modest Lydia."

"Well, you are one and the same, but let me give you a word of advice Miss Lydia. A true lady learns to accept compliments graciously."

"Does she really? Well it`s just as well I`m not a true lady isn`t it?" Lydia quickened her step. In two strides he was level with her again.

"Don`t lets quarrel, we`re only just getting to know one another. Besides, I wanted to thank you." They walked on, still occasionally passing stragglers from morning service walking in the opposite direction. Lydia knew they were all curious about the young gentleman walking beside her. It would not do to take his arm.

"Thank me, what for?"

"Your poem. I found it under my pillow."

"But that was meant for Alfred. A little welcome home poem, we...we exchange poems like that sometimes."

"Yes, Alfred told me all about it, such a lovely little habit. But you see I slept in his bed, so I got the poem!"

"But it wasn`t for you. But why should you care? A silly childish poem!" Lydia hurried on.

Jack took the poem from his notebook and read aloud

"Flower in the crannied wall
I pluck you out of the crannies,
I hold you here, root and all, in my hand,
Little flower... but if I could understand
What you are, root and all, all in all,
I should know what God and man is.`

"Tennyson again."

They were standing near the spot where the style led to the barley. This time he plucked a sprig of buttercups.

"Come; forgive me for keeping the poem. It was a jest at first, but I think it was fated for me. And besides..." He placed the poem back inside his jacket.

"Besides what?"

"Well, no-one has ever given me a poem."

She took the buttercups.

26

"I'll have you know that many a young lad has given me bunches of buttercups, and made daisy chains for my hair!"

"My, you've had admirers for years!"

"But we were just little children then... Oh, Jack Albright!"

They walked on companionably and she tucked the buttercups inside her bag. She had lost the poppy, she would treasure these.

"You may keep the poem," she said quietly.

Four

"Isn`t it splendid, Lydia? The Reverend Peabody has invited us to tea tomorrow," Eliza said as she and Lydia helped Polly put the finishing touches to the huge Sunday roast.

Lydia nearly dropped the roast potatoes. "Tea with the Reverend?"

"Yes, it`s all because of Jack of course. Class and bearing will out. People were falling over themselves to be introduced, surely you noticed, Lydia?"

"Well yes, but…"

"Yes, tea with the Reverend, a dinner invitation later in the week from Dr. Morton - your father was delighted about that – and most surprising of all, you young things have been invited to a tennis party at the Grange!" Eliza could hardly contain her excitement.

Lydia was pleased for her parents about Dr. Morton, but tennis at the Grange – why before today that would have been unthinkable! And tea at the Rectory made Lydia squirm inwardly.That awful Sunday afternoon six years previously flashed before her.

Reverend Peabody had just taken up the incumbency at St. John`s, when the family was invited to tea. She had detested twelve-year old Amelia Peabody on sight, with her frilly dress and nose in the air. When the cakes were handed round and Amelia had declined them, Lydia proceeded to stuff her face as fast as she could. To make matters worse their pet Pekinese had bitten her ankle, and Lydia kicked him. At home, her father had whacked her so hard she couldn't sit down for days. Needless to say, no further invitations had ever been forthcoming – until now.

Later at lunch, Alfred mentioned the invitation to the Grange for tennis.

"I can`t play, so I shan`t go," said Lydia, emphatically.

"We could teach you, Lyddy," said Alfred, "but we had planned to make our way to Cumberland on Saturday."

"We can put off leaving for a day or two, I`m sure," said Jack flashing Lydia a disarming smile.

"You`ll enjoy it, Lydia. Every young lady should learn how to play tennis."

While the parents slept off the huge lunch the two boys and Lydia went over to the school, to hunt out tennis racquets and balls.

"I doubt that we`ll get very far with these," frowned Alfred as he regarded the warped frames and missing catgut strings of several old racquets and a couple of scuffed balls. "Anyway, it`s too warm. Let`s go and have a swim."

Lydia`s heart sank, as she knew her father would disapprove of her swimming with the boys.

"Oh, come on these two aren`t too bad" Jack said bouncing a ball off one of the racquets. "Here, you have this one Lydia." She could have jumped for joy. The boys took off their jackets and ties, and Alfred sat in the shade as Jack and Lydia hit the ball gently between them in the schoolyard.

"Okay, so you can hit a ball Lydia, now let`s teach you how to hold the racquet properly. Like this for forehand, and this for backhand," he demonstrated, then hit a ball a little off her forehand. Lydia squealed as she tried to reach it and failed.

"Oh, it`s hopeless in these boots." She sat down next to Alfred and unbuttoned her boots, handing the racquet to her brother. He took it up, and the two boys began a spirited knock about in the limited space, Lydia laughing and clapping as their strokes got harder and wilder.

Jack beckoned her over. "Come and try this." He moved close behind her, his hand over hers, moving her arm backwards and forwards in the forehand movement, then demonstrating the backhand.

"Okay Alfie. Throw us a good ball; see if Lydia can get it back to you."

Alfred did, and Lydia returned it several times, or rather Jack did. Then he let go of her and stepped back. "Now try it on your own."

Lydia did her best, but her heart was beating so fast she found it hard to focus. She could still feel his strong arms and his breath on her cheek.

"For goodness sake concentrate!" Alfred shouted as he served her a wide backhand. They were all getting hot with the exercise, but Alfred looked crimson in the summer sun.

"Now, now patience dear boy. Come on, you can play us both." Jack tossed the ball to Lydia and she tried a serve.

They played for a while longer, the two boys having most of the game, with Lydia hitting the odd easy shot, encouraged by Jack. She began to relax and enjoy it, squealing with delight when she managed to return a ball, the boys barracking each other. Eventually the old ball split, so Jack gave it a mighty whack, sending over the wall to somewhere in the vicarage gardens, making Lydia scream with laughter.

"Lydia! Alfred! What on earth do you think you`re doing. All this noise! Have you forgotten it`s Sunday Afternoon?" Henry`s authoritative voice instantly silenced them all.

Alfred`s face grew even redder as he gathered up the racquets. "Sorry father – thought we could teach Lydia a few strokes for next week."

"I wish someone could teach the girl to grow up! Playing in your stocking feet Lydia. I hope you darn the holes yourself!"

"Of course father. Sorry father."

Henry stormed off, and Lydia went to put on her boots, not daring to look at Jack, she felt so humiliated. He followed and sat beside her.

"Oh dear. They will take some darning," he smiled as Lydia wiggled her toes on her left foot which were protruding from the black wool, and looking none too clean after scuffing about in the yard.

"This little piggy went to market, this little piggy stayed at home…" He gently touched the end of her toes one by one as he began the nursery rhyme. His touch sent tingles up her spine. She thrust her foot quickly into her boot.

"Jack Albright! Stop it!"

"Well your father said you`re still a baby, so baby rhymes would seem the thing."

Lydia was incensed. "I`m not a baby, I was just enjoying myself. How could I play in these boots?"

Jack put his hand firmly on her shaking fingers as she tried to do up her laces. "Don't be upset. That's fathers for you. You should see mine!"

They were both hot, and the front of Jack's shirt was damp. His black curls clung to his forehead from where a trickle of sweat ran into his eyes. Lydia resisted the urge to wipe it away as they looked into each other's eyes.

"And I know you're not a baby Lydia. You're all grown up, I can see that." He brushed a stray hair away from her damp forehead.

"Jack! Come on, I still fancy a swim. I'll get the towels. Lydia, I don't think you'd better come do you?" Alfred was back, looking cross.

She stood up and straightened her skirt. "Of course not. Look where having fun gets me. See you later." She strode off with her nose in the air, trying to conceal her hurt pride and trembling knees.

The boys missed tea, but Lydia was relieved, especially when she was castigated yet again for ruining her stockings. "Beyond repair," Eliza tutted.

She went to bed early and read her Tennyson by candlelight. Later, she heard the boys in garden as they chatted and laughed beneath the chestnut tree. How she longed to be with them, but she couldn't risk infuriating her father any more. Instead, she reflected on the day, particularly the time spent with Jack. How she had loved the tennis game - she couldn't remember the last time she had laughed so much, and she could still feel the warmth of Jack's body against hers, the touch of his strong hands, his fingers on her toes, on her forehead. She was sure he would have kissed her if Alfred hadn't turned up. She shivered with delight, and wrote in her journal

"Today is the happiest day of my life."

The boys went off into town the following day, for Alfred to shop for walking clothes for their holiday in Cumberland, as Lydia taught school as usual.

Later, they all trooped round to the vicarage for tea, Lydia once again wearing her dreaded pink rosebud dress which her mother had altered to fit her.

This time she smiled sweetly at Amelia, now accompanied by her younger sister Maude, but after a condescending nod in her direction, the girls spent all their time simpering and fluttering their eyelashes at Jack, whilst the adults made boring small talk. Eventually Mrs. Peabody coughed nervously. "Ahem, Amelia, Maude - why don't you take the young gentlemen - and Lydia, of course, for a little walk in the garden?"

Lydia and Alfred trailed behind Jack as he walked with Amelia and Maude either side of him around the garden. As they came to a rambling rose bush Jack plucked two pink roses and presented them to each of the sisters with a flourish. As they blushed and simpered, Lydia felt the colour rush to her own cheeks, as she fought to control a new emotion. What was he doing? How could he! Perhaps he would be comparing them to works of art next! She was just about to flounce off, when she saw the battered old ball that Jack had hit over the wall. She ran and retrieved it.

"Here Jack, catch!"

33

Her aim missed Jack and hit Amelia on the shoulder, who glared at her with pure hatred.

"Oops, so sorry Amelia," Lydia said in a flat voice.

"Lydia! Boys! Time to go!"

As they followed their proud parents back to School House, Alfred whispered angrily "nearly did it again sis!" Jack was frowning too, but Lydia flounced home with her nose in the air.

Fortunately, she didn`t have time to dwell on things as it was her evening for choir practice at the Institute where she met up with Lizzie. The boys had arranged to meet them afterwards for a stroll down the lane, but Lydia strode on ahead.

Jack soon caught up with her. "Lydia, what have I done to upset you?"

"Upset me? You must be mistaken Sir."

They walked on a few paces, well apart, in silence. "Was it the roses I gave to the Miss Peabodies?"

"Did you?"

"You know I did. Oh, Lydia, it was only to please them, a little gesture. I was just being polite."

"Of course you were." Lydia smiled at a passing neighbour who doffed his cap as he overtook them.

"I was a guest – we all were. I was merely giving a token gesture in thanks."

"No doubt you are well practiced at token gestures. I should know. I was the recipient of a buttercup." Lydia spat out the last word.

"But buttercups are more than tokens. After all I`m sure you gave yours with…" Jack hesitated… "with affection."

Clever Jack!

"Of course, and it was meant for my brother."

"But you said I could keep it." He touched his breast pocket. "I have it still, and the poem. Do you have mine?"

Lydia shrugged and waved as a pony and trap passed them.

"I think our flowers from crannied walls mean more to us than roses from the garden. After all, I was merely giving them what was already theirs."

They had reached the cottage gate, and Jack smiled as he held it open for her, and once more she felt a sweet, surge of ecstasy within her. It staunched the fire of jealousy, the sensation of which she had not enjoyed. And he said he had kept her buttercup.

In her bedroom later, Lydia looked at herself in the mirror and felt surprised that her familiar face stared back at her, for it had seemed to her all day that everyone must know that she was totally transformed, for she was in love, wasn't she?

She laid her sprig of buttercups on the next page in her journal, and covered them with a tiny piece of tissue paper.

Five

The following day was cloudy and dull. "Perfect for Sports practice", announced Henry. So in the afternoon, Lydia, Mr. Thwaite, and Miss Hodges the other school teachers marched over eighty children between the ages of five and eleven down Claines Lane towards the meadows surrounding the Grange.

Every year the Squire allowed the school use of one of his fields for their annual Sports Day at the end of July. Half the children were actually away – pea picking had started on the farms, and a few had gone down with measles. Nevertheless, Sports Day was looming and Henry insisted they get it over with. Jack thought it would be a jolly wheeze to help out, so they brought up the rear of the procession behind Henry, loaded down with wooden hoops and canes.

As he helped set out the running lanes with rope and canes in the field, Lydia thought Jack looked to be thoroughly enjoying himself. Then it suddenly hit her. He would only be here for four more days. He had only been here for three, and yet already life without him seemed unbearable. What would she do when he was gone.

The sports practice consisted mainly of girls` and boys` races according to age, and a relay for the older children. Then individuals could choose either bowling a hoop, a sack race and egg and spoon.

"Why not an obstacle race?" Jack suggested. He had noticed newly stacked bales of hay at the corner of the field. "We could use those. Come on Alfie boy."

So while Henry, Mr.Thwaite and Lydia organised the running races the two boys set up another course with skipping ropes, hay bales, and hoops. All the boys then tried their luck just for fun, Jack urging them on, helping the little ones climb the bales and urging others to leap higher or skip faster.

Lydia had never seen the children enjoy themselves so much, and it was so obvious that they adored the boys.

"Thank you so much for this Jack. Sports Day itself will never be so much fun."

"I've thoroughly enjoyed myself Miss Lydia." Jack paused to take off his jacket and handed it to her. "Besides," he said quietly "anything to spend time with you."

Lydia was relieved that her father was at the other end of the field, probably disapproving of the fact that Jack had divested himself of his jacket. As she blushed with pleasure she held tightly onto Jack's jacket which still held the warmth of his body.

"This was all Jack's idea you know - thought father would need some help," Alfred told Lydia as they all marched back to school tired but happy. "Thank heavens he suggested it. Goodness knows what I'd have done with him today. I keep expecting him to be bored to death."

*

On Wednesday, the boys took a train to Birmingham. Apparently Jack had been unable to find walking boots in Worcester. Whilst there, they had toured the art gallery and the conversation that evening had been about the collection of modern paintings displayed there.

Lydia listened wide-eyed as Jack and Alfred described paintings by some of the old Masters, and a collection by artists who called themselves `The Pre-Raphaelites`.

"I think Waterhouse may have been one of their number. You know, Lydia he painted the Lady of Shalott."

Lydia held her breath, hoping he would not elaborate in front of her father, and thankfully, he continued to talk about the Impressionists.

"You should see them, Lydia, particularly the work of Monet. I saw his work in London. Next time, we`ll take you to the galleries Lydia, during the school holidays – with your permission Sir."

Henry nodded and Lydia`s heart soared. He was talking about the future! "I should very much like to learn more about art."

In the evening the boys accompanied Lydia into Barbourne for her weekly First Aid meeting run by her friend Lizzie Chance who was a nurse. They waited for her until the class was over in the Vine Inn, and accompanied her home, and walking between her brother and Jack, Lydia felt yet again, as if she were the luckiest girl alive.

When they arrived home, Jack suggested Henry join them for a drink at the Mug Inn, and much to everyone`s surprise, he went, leaving Lydia alone with her mother

"What an exceptional young man Jack Albright is. Your brother is so lucky to have made such a friend. I knew he had charmed us all, even me, but to have had this effect on Henry." Eliza`s tone suddenly changed as she regarded her daughter.

"Lydia, I`m not very good at…at intimate conversation, as you well know, but … this has to be said."

Lydia sat wide-eyed.

"I have seen the way you and Jack look at each other." Eliza blurted out.

"But Ma ..." Lydia began to protest.

"He will be leaving at the end of the week, Lydia. It would be lovely to think he will always be Alfred`s friend. We have such hopes for Alfred..."

"What are you trying to say ma?"

"I … I just don`t want you to have hopes above your… beyond…"

"Hopes above my station!" Lydia said through clenched teeth.

"Well, perhaps I do! Lydia, Jack is Alfred`s friend, he is exceptionally broad minded and tolerant, he has fitted in with things here amazingly well. But he is from a different class. His father is a member of parliament, and I have no doubt that they are not as broad minded as Jack. Oh, what am I saying? My dear he is a charming young man with the common touch, and he is a visitor. Just bear that in mind."

For once Lydia didn`t know what to say. In one way it was as if her mother could see straight through her, but she couldn`t know how she really felt could she? She couldn`t know that she loved him. She patted her mother`s hands which were clasped tightly together as she sat looking at her with such an anxious expression.

"Don`t worry Ma. I know who I am. I won`t embarrass you, father or Alfred. I think I`ll go for a walk in the garden."

Eliza sighed. Jack Albright had only been with them for a few days, but like a benevolent whirlwind he had shaken them all up. Shy, withdrawn Alfred seemed a different boy since meeting Jack. His confidence had blossomed, and the reticent country boy was becoming a sophisticated gentleman under Jack's influence. But with regard to Lydia she just had to hope that Jack Albright was every inch the gentleman he purported to be. Thank goodness he would be leaving soon

*

Lydia sat on the swing, but was in no mood for throwing out her legs and swinging for joy. She looked at the darkening sky, and spoke to the lone star she could see.

"I love Jack, I love Jack, and I think he loves me, but my mother is trying to tell me it can never be! Oh, being in love is such torture!"

*

There were even fewer children in school the following day, due to the measles epidemic and Henry decided to catch up on some paperwork at home. Lydia had never known him do this, but thought no more of it until she returned home herself after locking the school at the end of the day.

In the kitchen her father was sitting with a broad grin on his face, and she could hear the boys laughing in the back yard.

"They've taken the tub under the water pump, and are washing out there. Can you believe it? Jack has probably got a bathroom at home, he must think us so primitive." Nevertheless her mother was

40

saying this in a light-hearted fashion as she emptied a fishing basket of several plump specimens.

"They took your father fishing this afternoon. Freddie Maycroft took them to the Slip in his cart, and as you can see we have plenty for supper."

"Yes. yes, it was a very productive and enjoyable afternoon." Then Henry eyed Lydia meaningfully over his glasses. "But it's something, of course that we must keep to ourselves."

"Of course, Father."

"I think, however, that my old hobby could be revived." He coughed. "If this weather keeps up, perhaps next weekend, we three could go for a picnic. Would you enjoy that Lydia?"

Lydia could hardly believe her ears. "Oh, father that would be lovely."

It was all lovely, everything Jack touched was lovely. Her father playing truant, she couldn't believe it!

She joined her mother at the table under the window to gut the fish. She found that by leaning forward she could get the occasional glimpse of the boys as they washed. They had stripped down to their underpants, and were soaking wet. Jack suddenly came into full view as he tried to dodge Alfred who threw a bucket of water over him.

Lydia had seen pictures of Greek statues, and gleaming wet in the sunlight, Jack seemed to her every inch an Adonis, and he took her breath away. She had seen Alfred and the village boys larking around in the river in their drawers before, but suddenly this was very different. A surge of longing threatened to overwhelm her.

41

"Lydia! Take care, you'll cut yourself." Eliza took the knife off her and dispatched her to make tea.

*

It was another warm, June evening, and after supper the boys and Lydia went out to sit under the chestnut tree, taking a candle lantern and cushions with them. Jack had suggested that they read some poetry.

"We're off to the lakes, dear boy, let's remind ourselves of what the poets said about them," he said slapping Alfred on the back.

The boys were sitting on the old wooden tree-seat and Lydia settled herself at their feet with her little pile of books, and she watched, rapt as the two most beautiful boys in the world eloquently brought the lyrics and stanzas of the poets to life.

They took it in turn to read verses from "The Prelude", which Jack said was undoubtedly Wordsworth's masterpiece. By the end of it Alfred was yawning.

"Sorry you two, but I've had my fill of Wordsworth for one evening." Alfred gave a desultory wave, as he ambled off to the house. Jack patted the seat beside him, and Lydia dutifully sat down where Alfred had been. Jack's closeness made her heart beat faster, and to her relief, he edged away, lifting one leg onto the seat, his back supported by its rickety arm, so that he was facing her.

Jack still held the book open as if he were reading, but instead said "How lovely it would be if you could accompany us to Cumberland."

42

"Oh, yes, it would be great fun, but sadly it cannot be. What shall we read next?" Lydia fought to make her voice sound level.

"May I write to you? I shall describe everything we see. I may even compose my own poetry." He laughed, "… although I doubt it."

"Oh, Jack! I'm sure you could do anything if you put your mind to it!"

"Dear, sweet, Lydia. If only you knew how difficult I find it to put my mind to anything – especially when looking at you." He paused, and Lydia held her breath. "We are in full view of the house, and illuminated for all to see, and I think it is just as well."

"And why is that?" Lydia teased.

"I should like to loosen your hair again, and touch your dear cheek."

The two of them locked eyes in the heavy, scented night air.

Lydia forgot all about social conventions, what could or couldn't be. Her mother was wrong about Jack, he loved her. She lost herself in the moment, treasuring every second of the here and now.

"Lydia! Jack!" Eliza called from the kitchen doorway. "Don't leave the cushions out there to get damp."

They exchanged a loving look. Something had passed between them which had not needed words.

They gathered up the cushions and books, and Jack led Lydia back to the house, holding the lantern aloft. The kitchen door was ajar, but the lamp within had been extinguished. They stood close together in the doorway. Their arms were full of cushions and books, and Jack lowered his face to hers. His lips briefly brushed hers. He drew away quickly and sighed. Then he turned and quickly walked away, taking the light with him.

Lydia stood motionless in the darkness. She waited, willing him to come back, yearning for the touch of Jack`s lips on hers. But he didn`t return.

Six

The next morning Dr. Morton called at School House.

"This measles epidemic is quite wearing me out Mrs. Winters, and I have several more calls to make," he explained to Eliza. "Unfortunately my youngest girls are sick too, so I`m afraid I shall have to postpone our dinner invitation this evening. But you must come as soon as the girls have recovered."

Eliza had felt cheered by his visit. There had once been a genuine friendship between the doctor and Henry that had cooled of late. Eliza knew that it was because the doctor`s good wife had shown her disapproval of Henry`s partaking of too much wine at their last dinner party. She would ensure that he would not repeat the mistake.

Jack and Alfred went fishing on their own that day, and had returned just as Lydia arrived home from school. The evening was heavy and sultry, so after a rubber of whist, Jack and Alfred wandered off for a walk, saying they might call in at the Mug. Lydia felt left out, knowing that there would not be many more times she and Jack could be together. Tomorrow was the tennis party, which she was dreading.

As if she read her mind Eliza said "I have a surprise Lydia. I found this smart piece of white gabardine that I've made into a skirt for you. And I`m told plimsolls are quite the fashion for young ladies playing tennis."

Lydia was overcome. She hugged her mother and thanked her. Well at least she would not look too much the pauper. Harriet and Edwin Bengeworth would no doubt have other smart upper class friends there, and she had dreaded she would look, literally, like the village idiot.

*

At the pub there were a few locals, who touched their forelocks as Jack and Alfred took their mugs of ale outside.

"You have remembered this wretched tennis party tomorrow haven`t you?" said Alfred.

"Oh, yes, the tennis party. Well Lydia will be looking forward to it, and we did teach her a thing or two." Jack smiled and drank deeply. "Cheer up old boy, it won't be that bad will it?"

"We`ve only been invited because of you. Still, more up your street than all this fishing and walking I suppose."

"But I've really enjoyed being here in this little neck of the woods."

"But every day, I was convinced you would announce that you wanted to leave; that you were bored to tears…"

"No, dear friend. I can`t tell you how pleasant it has been to spend time with a close family; with you. As I said, I have never known it."

Jack gazed over at the church, and Alfred sensed he was serious. "Well, I`ll have you know, that you have helped to bring out the best in father. I suppose I am the blue-eyed boy, and Lydia has a devil of a job to please him. She`s always been the fearless, spirited one, characteristics I wish I possessed, but which father can`t seem to abide in her. We`re not really what we seem, Jack. Mother married beneath her and Father finds it hard to live with the guilt."

Jack shrugged "Still seems a happy family compared to mine. I just feel so for Lydia. I have become very fond of her Alfred."

"I was afraid of that."

"Why afraid? Don't worry, she shall be my friend; she is my best friend's sister, and I shall write to her when we go to Cumberland. I think we should leave tomorrow."

"But we have the tennis party, remember? Lydia will be so disappointed."

"And you?" Jack lifted an eyebrow.

"Well, it would have been nice to be welcomed at the Squire's home. It would have made mother so proud."

"Very well, if you insist. But I fear it will be another ordeal for dearest Lydia."

Jack placed his empty tankard into Alfred' s hand.

*

Lydia had found it hard to sleep. It was a close, humid evening and she thought she heard thunder in the distance. Then she heard the boys returning, making more noise than surely was necessary. After a while she heard footsteps on the stairs and saw the passing light of a candle under her door.

She must have dropped off, but was woken by the crash of thunder. She wasn't in the least afraid of storms; in fact she enjoyed them. Another reason for her parents to shake their heads in disbelief at her. She lit her candle and stood at her window. A jagged bolt of lightning lit up the back garden like daylight. She had a ridiculous thought that it would be nice to go out and dance in the rain.

"Lydia!" She thought she was hearing things, but there was Jack, standing beneath her window, and beckoning for her to join her.

"Come on, it's wonderful down here!"

She went soundlessly down the stairs, took her father's umbrella from the stand and tip-toed out into the back garden. Another flash of lightning illuminated everything, including Jack, soaked to the skin. He was barefooted, bare headed and in his shirt sleeves. Lydia suddenly felt self-conscious in her white lawn nightdress, even though she was covered from top to toe.

She indicated for him to come inside. "Jack! You'll catch your death of cold! Are you drunk?"

"Yes, very probably." He laughed. "Come and stand here with me. It's not cold in the least! Come and tempt the gods to do their worst!"

Lydia walked over to him, still holding the umbrella, and tried to hold it over his head. "Come on in, you silly boy!"

"It's too late for that Lydia." He held her close, took the umbrella from her and tossed it aside.

"Jack, I think you're a little drunk"

"Not drunk, Lady Lydia, intoxicated. Intoxicated by you."

Lydia could hardly believe her ears. She felt a thrill of excitement, but something told her to keep her head. It was the drink talking. She must humour him, get him back inside, but he resisted when she tried to lead him towards the house.

"Very well, then, let's dance. I've always wanted to dance in the rain." She took both his hands and they turned round in circles, sloshing in the puddles already covering the grass, Jack almost falling over. The lightning flashed and the thunder crashed, almost simultaneously.

"A gentleman should hold a lady like this when they dance." Jack pulled her towards him and they attempted to waltz. Jack overbalanced and they fell to the ground. Soon his lips were devouring her, and Lydia could think of nothing but the urgency and sweetness of his rain drenched kisses. Her arms were around his broad shoulders, and she felt his hardness and urgency as his body pressed against her. Oh, what was happening? There was another great clap of thunder and the simultaneous lightning illuminated his face as he leant back to gaze down at her.

"Oh God, Lydia I want you so." His hands caressed her breasts and their lips met again. Last night she had wanted these kisses so much, now a voice in her head was saying `not like this, not like this…`

She pushed Jack away, and wriggled free.

"No, Jack! What are you doing?"

There was another flash of lightening and a longer gap before the thunder. The storm was moving away. Lydia could hear Jack`s heavy breathing, then he was suddenly on his feet and helping her up.

He kissed her hand, and held it to his breast with both of his. "Dear Lydia, oh, darling girl, I`m so sorry. Please forgive me."

Lydia reached out with her other hand and touched his cheek as the rain now beat down steadily. "Please come in out of the rain."

They stood outside the back door between the kitchen and scullery where the roof shielded them. Lydia couldn't stop shaking, and Jack held her close.

"I love you, Lydia, marry me. I wanted to kiss you the first time I saw you – when you hugged Alfred I wished it was me. No-one has ever made me feel like you do. I`m sorry I got so… so carried away, but surely you feel it too, Lydia?"

She blushed as she recalled his body against her, his hands on her body. "Yes, Jack. I love you, but marriage, you and I?"

"That`s what people do when they're in love. Marry me!"

"Oh, yes, Jack, yes!"

As they hugged, the rain stopped abruptly. The shaking had stopped and Lydia felt a warm glow of contentment as they gazed out at the dark sky, where tiny pin-pricks of stars began to appear.

Jack kissed her gently then whispered;

"`As often through the purple night
Below the starry clusters bright
Some bearded meteor, trailing light,
Moves over still Shalott.`".

Meteors are said to appear at momentous times. There should be one now."

Lydia recalled the first night and how that very verse from The Lady of Shalott had captivated her.

"Come, we must go in. Your father mustn`t find us."

At the mention of her father, Lydia suddenly crashed back to earth. She told Jack to take off his clothes, and giggled softly as she turned her back.

"I shall have to hide them in the wash house. Don't worry, I'll sort it out in the morning." There was just enough light from the candle she had left in the kitchen to see the glistening curve of his shoulders, as he turned his back towards her.

"We must go to bed now. Be careful Jack."

Jack blew out the candle, and reached for her in the darkness. "Goodnight little lady. You must keep our secret for now. Our special, wonderful secret."

They clung together in one final embrace, as Jack stroked her helmet of wet hair, then she pushed him from her. "Go, my darling, please go."

She left Jack to tip toe up to his bed, then Lydia stripped off her own wet, muddy nightdress. She then screwed their wet clothes into a bundle and hid them in the basket of the washhouse under the pile of laundry waiting for Monday morning. She remembered doing this after an illicit swim with the village boys in the river years ago. But this was different; she was no longer that child.

It was her turn to tiptoe up the stairs. She had just reached her room and was about to close the door when she heard her mother on the tiny landing.

"Lydia? Are you alright? I thought I heard noises."

Lydia opened her door a fraction.

"The storm woke me, mother. I went down to get a drink of water."

"Yes, it woke me too. I marvel at you Lydia, no fear at all. Your father slept through it all as usual. Well, goodnight."

Lydia breathed a huge sigh of relief. She found herself a clean nightgown and sat at her open window looking out onto place on the lawn where they had been Jack had been drunk, she knew that, and his urgency had frightened her a little, as had her own passion, for she had wanted him too. He had asked her to marry him, but she understood why for now it must be a secret. She was not a sophisticated woman, but she knew that there would have to be a courtship, permission obtained from parents. Could a girl like her marry a boy like him? She had a feeling that it would not be easy for Jack, but surely her own would be pleased if Jack offered marriage, in spite of what her mother had said to her earlier. But for now she would keep their love a secret.

She had written of the day's events in the diary earlier. She could never find words to express how she felt at the moment, so she wrote simply - *'Tonight I am a Woman,'* and she sat in her window staring a long time at the starry clusters bright. Jack loved her, he wanted to marry her. Somehow they could make it happen. She gazed out at the starry sky. The storm had passed.

Seven

Seated at the breakfast table, the next morning Lydia felt that she was surrounded by some kind of aura; she felt sure that everyone could see the difference in her. She was astonished that Jack looked the same, and she was almost afraid to look at him in case she betrayed her emotions. But he had barely glanced at her when he had said `Good Morning`. She was relieved when her mother said Henry had stayed in bed.

"The heavy weather gave him a migraine which has not abated with the storm." She peered at Alfred and Jack. "You boys look a little green round the gills, too."

"Yes, well I took Jack to the Mug last night" yawned Alfred.

"I`m not used to such strong country ale, Mrs.Winters." Jack sipped his tea.

Eliza looked outside. "It`s still raining. I hardly think you`ll be playing tennis today. My goodness, what`s that?"

"Why it`s an umbrella Mrs. Winters," said Polly, peering through the kitchen window. Jack and Lydia exchanged glances.

"An umbrella? Oh, my goodness, I remember now," said Jack jumping up. "I used it last night. I`ll get it at once." He ran out into the back garden, retrieved the umbrella which had obviously been blowing about the garden all night, and popped it inside the wash- house to dry out.

"I`m sorry, I couldn`t sleep last night – the storm you`ll remember – I say what a storm! Well, anyway,

I quite like storms, so I took the umbrella, and had a walk in the garden." Everyone stared at Jack as though he were mad. He shrugged and continued. "Well, I'm afraid in spite of the umbrella I still got wet, thoroughly soaked in fact. I got so wet that I left my clothes in the wash house. My apologies Polly."

"That's alright Sir. I'll have them washed, but they'll take some drying today."

"The umbrella? How did you forget about the umbrella?" asked Eliza.

"Oh, it must have been when I had a swing," replied Jack, quick as a flash.

"A swing?" said Alfred and Eliza in unison.

"Yes. I distinctly remember swinging. I'm so sorry about the umbrella. I think a spoke may be broken. I'll leave money for it to be repaired. I say Polly, this porridge is deliciously creamy."

Polly shot Lydia another amused glance. "You're welcome Sir."

Just as Lydia started breathing normally again – it seemed as if she had been holding her breath for ages – some-one rapped on the front door.

Alfred went to answer it and returned holding an envelope.

"That was Stepford from The Grange. The tennis party has been cancelled, which will come as no surprise, I'm sure. He's left this though. Mother." Alfred handed Eliza an envelope, which she opened in awe.

"Why, it's an invitation. "To Mr. and Mrs. Winters, Alfred, Lydia and Mr. Jack Albright Esq. It's an invitation to their Summer Ball!"

"When is it?" asked Alfred.

"Saturday, 2nd August." Eliza looked from one face to another, full of expectation.

"Well, I'll be home by then. But we all know it's Jack's presence they want."

"Then they shall have me! Mrs. Winters, please accept on my behalf. I shall return to Claines for the Ball- if I may presume on your hospitality again?"

Lydia clapped her hands in delight. The Squire's summer ball! And Jack was coming back for it! Visions of a light, music and twirling dancers filled her head, visions and images she only knew from books. And, she would be dancing with Jack – Jack who wanted to marry her!

"In the meantime… Alfred I think we should leave for the Lakes today as we originally planned. It's only drizzling now; far too wet for tennis, but perfect for travelling. Polly, will you run down the lane and see if young Freddie will take us to the tram, say in about an hour?"

Lydia couldn't believe what she was hearing.

Jack appeared oblivious to the shocked expression on everyone's faces. Eventually Alfred said "I know the tennis party has been cancelled but you told me that you weren't that keen on tennis anyway."

"Not really, but you know I really think I might get on everyone's nerves if I hang about much longer – don't want to overstay my welcome!" Jack pushed away his plate and patted his stomach. "And all this wonderful food Mrs.Winters! Don't look so shocked Alfred! I say, why don't you let me go ahead, and you can join me at Windermere when you're ready."

Alfred stood up. "No, no Jack. We'll leave together, as originally planned."

Lydia sat in stunned silence. She watched as the two boys left the room. Since his first greeting, Jack had not looked at her once.

Eliza had noticed. "Such a shame, but never mind, you have the Ball to look forward to."

In reply Lydia left her seat and put on her bonnet and cape. "I'm going to catch Polly up. I need to walk."

By the time she reached Polly in the lane, tears were streaming down Lydia's face. She didn't know what she would have done if she had had to moment longer.

"Whatever's the matter, Miss Lydia?" asked Polly stopping and taking her arm.

Lydia shook her off.

"Oh don't stop, I have to walk, I feel like screaming!" Instead she sobbed aloud. "I hate him, I hate him!"

"No need for me to ask who you 'ates!" Polly bustled beside her.

"Last night he said he loved me. He asked me to marry him! He promised a downy white, marriage bed!"

"Oh, Miss you didn't!"

Lydia stopped and looked at her. "Didn't what?"

"Well, make do with, I dunno, a grassy bed? Them wet clothes an' all…"

"No Polly! We danced. We danced in the rain, in the storm, we felt part of the elements" – Lydia threw her arms dramatically into the air. "And today

56

he …he kissed me, Polly, he held me – oh! I love him, I love him!"

"A minute ago you `ated `im!"

"I hate him too! After …after…after kissing me like that, this morning he barely looked at me, and then he announced that he was leaving. Oh, Polly, I can`t bear it! How can I live without him?"

They had reached the stile that led to the barley field and memories of that first night, that first walk came flooding back to her. She sat down on the wooden step and wept as if her heart would break.

Polly let her cry. She resisted the urge to say she had thought all along it would end in tears.

"Come on, now Miss. Folks`ll be about soon and they`ll wonder what`s up. `Ere blow yer nose."

Lydia eventually stood up and they trudged on in silence. She turned her face to the rain. The cool, kind drops comforted her a little. Then instantly, she remembered the tumultuous downpour of last night. She frowned as she heard Polly trying to suppress a giggle.

"I can`t think what there is to laugh at!"

"I`m sorry Miss. It`s them feet of yourn in yer mam`s boots. They`m miles too big and they turns up at the toes like a clown!"

Lydia looked down at her mother`s boots. She had slipped them on in haste, and they were too big for her. Polly was right. Her feet looked really comical, and in spite of herself she smiled. Another time she would have had Polly in fits by doing a funny walk, but she had no heart for that today.

"But Miss you`ve got ter carry on. My mam says that men are put on this earth to give sorrow and trials to us women. You only have to look at `er and me dad to know that`s true enough!"

Lydia smiled then stopped. They had reached the Maycroft`s cottage.

"Saints alive! It`s old Fred on at poor Freddie again!

"I`ll swing for you one of these days! Gerrout thur and get some trade!" Fred senior growled at his son, and the two girls clung to each other as they watched poor Freddie being man-handled out of the door by his father. "And don`t come back `til you`ve earned yer keep!"

Freddie staggered to stop himself from falling.

"Don`t let him see us, Polly" whispered Lydia, and they retraced their steps to the wall in front of Taffy Jones` Smithy. They could still hear the shouting going on between husband and wife in the cottage.

"He`s a brute that Fred Maycroft, and her`s as bad. Always rowin`, and poor old Freddie, he wouldn`t hurt a fly. Still full of the drink from last night in the Mug."

"Polly, you and Freddie – you`re not…"

"Huh! Chance `ud be a fine thing. `ow could we go courting` when neither of `em`ll let `im out of their sight?" How could Lydia not know about her and Freddie? Too wrapped up in herself, that`s why! Polly thought.

They could hear the chink of the harness from the tumbledown stable, and soon Freddie was walking old Bessie out harnessed to the cart.

"`Mornin` Freddie," Polly said cheerfully and walked up to him as Lydia stroked old Bessie`s head.

58

"Bit of a damp `un, ladies" smiled Freddie. "What brings you down `ere then?"

"Alfred and his guest are leaving us, Freddie. Could you take them to pick up the tram in Barbourne, say in about an hour?" Lydia marvelled at Freddie`s composure.

"`Course I can, and I`ll take you back `ome now."

"Take Polly, Freddie I need to walk."

"You alright Miss? Looks like you bin cryin`"

"I...I slipped on the wet floor in the washhouse, and hurt my ankle. You know what a baby I am Freddie," she smiled.

"Yes, I remember you squealing when we stung ourselves on them nettles!"

"Yes, and who was it who fetched the dock leaves for me?"

"Yes, funny how you was such a babby with the little things, but it never stopped you - always ready to get back into the fray you was!" They smiled the smiles of a shared memory, as Polly pursed her lips and climbed into the cart.

"Lairy mare," she muttered to herself. She knew that Freddie had always carried a candle for her. Well, it was time he blew out that flame! Her and Freddie would make a good pair - he was hardworking and she knew he liked her well enough. O.K. he had that funny foot, but she was no oil painting. `Ginger Nut`, all the kids had called her, like they had tormented him with `cripple`, but it was water off a duck`s back. If they were married, they could work as a couple at the Grange, live in, have a bit of a future away from `is folks. It wasn`t so bad with the Winters, true, but Lydia was starting to get on her nerves. All her flighty ways, pretending they were equals. And what did she think she was doing, throwing herself at Master Jack? It was as stupid as her hoping Alfred would look at her! She'd end up in trouble, that one and no mistake! Needs summat to cry for, she does!

Lydia had composed herself when she got back to the cottage. The boys were playing draughts at the kitchen table. Alfred looked up and asked about their lift, but Jack seemed very absorbed in his next move.

"I can come with you to the station, can't I - Alfred, Jack?" Lydia looked straight into Jack's eyes but he was the first to look away, and Lydia's heart sank.

"Of course you can, Lyddy," smiled Alfred.

At the station, Jack pecked her on the cheek. "Goodbye Lydia. Thanks for being such fun this week." She grasped his arm in fury.

"Fun? I was fun was I?" She gave a mock little curtsy and said in mock dialect. "So glad I was able to oblige, you Sir!"

"Lydia, keep your voice down! What's the matter with you?" hissed Alfred.

"Ask him, ask his Lordship what's the matter with me?"

Jack paused. "Alfred, kiss your sister goodbye"

Alfred looked from his sister to Jack. "What's going on here, Jack? Lydia, why are you upset?"

Lydia tossed her head and turned away. Jack took Alfred's arm. "Get on the train Alfred. I'll explain. Give me a moment with Lydia, please."

"Lydia, is there something you need to tell me?" Alfred stood his ground.

"It`s alright Alfred, really. Do as Jack says."

Alfred picked up his bags and walked on, glancing back uneasily.

"Why?" asked Lydia looking into Jack`s eyes and fighting back the tears. Why have you been unable to look at me all day? I feel shamed. Last night, last night I was in heaven, today you have cast me into hell!"

Jack smiled, pulled her towards him and kissed her forehead. "Dear, sweet, melodramatic Lydia."

She struck him on the chest and pushed him away. "Don`t patronise me like a child, like a plaything! But then, that`s probably what I am to you!"

He grasped her shoulders tightly. "Oh, if only you knew what you are to me! I meant it Lydia, I love you." He held her closely once more

"… but you must understand … I can`t marry you…"

I knew it!" Lydia struggled against his embrace.

"I can`t marry you YET! I can`t just ride off with you like Lancelot on a white charger. I have to go on this holiday, I have to go home and speak to my father. And Lydia," - he looked into her eyes, "I know what he will say. He will insist I finish university and my studies. He will tell me to wait. And we must wait – I should have waited before declaring my feelings."

"Please don`t regret last night. Please don`t make me feel shame."

Jack cupped her face in his hands. "Poor Lydia. What have I done to you? That's exactly what I felt like this morning, ashamed. I couldn't look at you, I had to go. My darling, don't you realise I just want to take you in my arms every time I see you? I know I can't, and I can't bear it. Lydia, I have never been in love before. The thought of marriage had never entered my head, and now ... well now everything has changed. Please forgive me, my darling."

Lydia spoke through her tears. "I'll forgive you Jack. I'll forgive you if you promise that one day... I can wait Jack. I can wait forever. I love you so!"

"My dear sweet girl. You won't have to wait forever."

They could hear the porter's whistle.

"The train won't wait forever." He held her hand and they ran up the tiled steps to the platform. Alfred was standing with the train door open.

Jack took Lydia once more in his arm and kissed her long and passionately.

"I'll write," he shouted as he jumped onto the train and slammed the door. The porter blew his whistle and waved his flag. The huge engine started up and she was soon wreathed in clouds of steam. Lydia stood waving long after the train had snaked out of sight, her lips still burning from Jack's kiss.

Eight

"Don`t look at me like that, old boy" Jack said.

Alfred looked furious as he flung himself down in the opposite seat. Not for the first time he felt at a distinct disadvantage in their relationship.

"What have you done to my sister, Jack?" Alfred`s face was grim. Jack leant towards him, and put his hand on his knee. He held his stare.

"I love your sister, Alfred, and she loves me. I never meant for this to happen. God knows, I never dreamt…"

Alfred shook his hand away.

"Never meant for what to happen?"

"I love Lydia and she loves me. Last night, after you went to bed, we … we talked and … well, declared our love for each other!"

"You`re incredible Jack Albright! I could see the two of you were attracted, but how can you fall in love with someone after a few days? And she`s so young. You can`t just play with her affections like this, Jack! For heaven`s sake man, she`s little more than a child!"

"Of course to you she may seem so, but she`s a young woman, Alfred; a lovely young woman!"

Alfred stood up, and pulled Jack up by his shoulders. He threw a punch, the force of which Jack managed to deflect. A sudden jolt of the points as the train began to slow, threw them together onto the seat. The compartment door opened.

"Is everything alright, gentlemen?"

They both looked up at a burly guard who coughed and examined his watch. "Next stop Bromsgrove!" he announced then closed the door.

Jack looked at Alfred and burst out laughing. Alfred straightened his tie and resumed his seat opposite.

"Everything's a joke to you. I suppose I'm a joke. I'll bet this past week has been a joke – something to laugh about with your crowd back at Oxford." He leant forward as the train pulled into the station. "But mark my words, I'll not have you making fun of Lydia. I'll not have it Jack!"

"I assure you it's the last thing on my mind." Jack held Alfred's furious stare. "You have to believe me; I'm serious about Lydia. I love Lydia, and you Alfie, you're the best friend a man could have."

"Be honest with me Jack. What has happened between you and Lydia?"

"We've kissed Alfred. Last night, in the rain, I took her in my arms, and we kissed that's all, but I knew. Lydia is extraordinary. I can't explain to you, her brother. But she feels like… like the other half of me. Last night, it felt like we could have held hands and together, we could have run away and conquered the world! But we had to make do with dancing in the rain."

"But this morning you couldn't get away fast enough. I don't believe you."

"Of course you don't. You've never been in love. Neither have I until now. Look, Alfred, I am only too aware of the differences between us. I wish they didn't exist, but they do. This morning, in the cold light of day, I couldn't look at Lydia for fear of betraying my emotions. I asked her to marry me, but I had no right to until I had spoken with my father, and of course, your father. But I will. I am determined that we shall be together. I will speak to my father after our holiday and convince him I mean to marry Lydia."

Alfred gave a derisive snort. "And how will you do that?"

"I don`t know, old boy, but I mean to do it. I promised Lydia and I promise you. You must believe me."

His voice broke with emotion. Alfred had never seen his friend so serious.

"Very well, Jack. I just can`t bear to think of little Lydia with a broken heart."

"I shan`t break her heart Alfred. But have you thought that she may break mine?"

Alfred looked at Jack`s handsome face, now smiling and confident again. No, it had never occurred to him that anyone could break his heart.

*

Hours later, the guard returned to inform them that the next stop was Manchester.

Jack looked out at the persistent rain. "You know, this is no weather to go fell walking. How do you fancy stopping off at Manchester? I think I told you that my father`s family live there, haven`t seen my cousins for ages. It`s Saturday, we could have dinner and maybe a night at the theatre. How about it? Cheer us both up, eh?"

Alfred`s heart sank. Dinner and theatre meant evening dress, and he only possessed walking and day clothes. He stared at the grey sky and the sodden landscape. "It may clear up by the time we get to Manchester."

"Now you are joking! It always rains in Manchester. Yes, that`s what we`ll do. Trust me, you`ll enjoy it. Now, cheer up my dear, serious friend. This is the start of our holiday, remember?"

Soon they were travelling in a hansom cab through the crowded streets of Manchester. This was a great city built on trade - wool and cotton, and the grand imposing buildings of the city centre reflected its affluence. The cabbie expertly guided his horse through the busy city centre, negotiating more motor-cars than Alfred had seen before. It amazed him that the horses, which were still in abundance, didn`t shy and bolt when they ostentatiously sounded their horns.

At The Palace Hotel, which Jack had obviously stayed at before, Alfred felt in awe of the opulent surroundings, wondering just what he was doing here, wondering if he would ever fit into Jack`s world. And if he thought that about himself, what about Lydia?

"Come on, old boy, I've run you a bath! Everything`s arranged! Dinner, then the music hall!"

Alfred looked up to see that Jack had hooked a dinner suit over the wardrobe door.

"Jack I can`t keep accepting your generosity …"

"I've just accepted yours for a week. Don`t be such a bloody bore. It`s too wet to go walking, relax and enjoy yourself!"

Alfred had felt so out of his depth since arriving at the hotel. He had little money of his own, Jack had always funded their adventures in Oxford - had even taken him with him on country house weekends with his friends. He had learned about fine wines and dining etiquette. It was an exciting, seductive world, but one he had not been born to, and he still felt an outsider, something Jack would never understand.

"I`m sorry Jack. Like you say, I`m a country bumpkin with no style. But who knows, when I put on that suit, I may pass muster!"

Whatever reservations he had, Alfred put to one side. His original ambition had been to become a solicitor, and he had proved himself to be so academically brilliant at Oxford that many, including Jack, had told him that he had the potential to one day take silk. But he was well aware that academic achievement alone would never be enough. It was the way of that world that it was who you knew as much as what you knew. Alfred knew that social connections were everything, and he was damned lucky to be making them with a genuine friend.

*

They dined at the hotel, and were joined by Jack`s two cousins, Ada and Emily. They were sisters and as different as chalk and cheese. Ada was tall and imposing with almost masculine features. She regarded Alfred from beneath her dark, hooded eyes, then smiled broadly, revealing large, horsy teeth.

"So you`re Alfred, Jack`s clever little friend! Delighted to meet you!"

Jack had told Alfred that Ada, unmarried at thirty eight, and therefore deemed to the `on the shelf`, devoted her life to good works and women`s suffrage. Alfred could imagine her putting the fear of

God into the Establishment. She put the fear of God into him. Emily, on the other hand, was small, shy and demure, with dimples in her cheek when she smiled. There was a likeness between her and her older sister, but Emily's features, were a little softer – her smile revealed small even teeth, and her tawny eyes sparkled in the candlelight. She was no beauty, but Alfred found himself captivated by her fragile charm. He had to strain to hear her voice when she spoke, which was very little, as Ada commanded the floor.

"… the mills continue to flourish of course, and at last my brothers listen to me a little more with regard to the workers' welfare." Ada was talking about the cotton mills her family owned, the main source of Jack's family wealth.

"From what mother tells me you keep an eye on everyone's welfare," Jack smiled.

"One has to do one's bit."

Emily leaned towards Alfred. "Ada is far too modest. She is completely tireless in her work for the poor. She has set up a home for fallen women, works tirelessly for an orphanage, not to mention the Red Cross organisation and her dedication to women's suffrage."

"It is the duty of the privileged classes to do what they can." She took a sip of wine and pulled a face. "Too dry, I think. No matter. As I said, Jack, I shall be after you to contribute to my causes before you leave."

Jack laughed. "And you, Emily dear? How do you fill your time?"

"Oh, Emily does her bit, don`t you dear? But unfortunately she has not been in the rudest of health just lately. However, seeing you Jack – and your fine friend here – has definitely put a bloom on her cheeks! Now, Alfred, tell me about Worcester. Tell me about your family, and your dear sister Jack has mentioned."

This woman doesn`t miss much, Alfred thought. He did tell the ladies about his family and his sister who had just qualified as a teacher.

"And is your clever sister pretty, Alfred?" asked Emily.

"Well yes. Jack thinks she looks like the Lady of Shalott, don`t you Jack?"

"Indeed! The Lady of Shalott!" Ada exclaimed, and for a second, Jack looked lost for words.

"Yes, that … that famous painting by Waterhouse where she is seated in the boat. You must know the one."

"Yes, I think I do, Jack. My word she must be a beauty!"

Jack deftly changed the subject, and Alfred thought once more that cousin Ada was a very astute woman indeed.

He felt immensely proud as Emily took his arm as they left the restaurant. What a good thing that Jack had arranged this diversion.

At the Alhambra theatre they watched an eclectic mix of cheeky male comedians, ballet dancers, a tight-rope and tumbling act, can-can dancers and the top of the bill was `The Norwegian Nightingale`. They all enjoyed it tremendously. Emily giggled and clapped everything with enthusiasm, and whenever

69

he could, Alfred stole a glance at her charming profile.

He couldn`t believe that they were the same two fellows who a few evenings ago had been sitting in the garden with Lydia reading Wordsworth.

Nine

Back at School House, Lydia paused as she helped Polly make the beds. She looked down the garden. Had it been there, only last night, that she had experienced the most important moments of her life? How was she going to carry on as if nothing had happened? She went into her own room with Jack`s pillow-case under her apron. She held it to her face and drank in the scent of him, and for a few seconds she was in ecstasy. As she slipped it under her own pillow she found a folded piece of paper.

> *"To My Lady Lydia.*
> *`I never saw so sweet a face*
> *As that I stood before*
> *My heart has left its dwelling place*
> *And can return no more -`*
> *John Clare says it for me.*
> *Until we meet again. – Always and Forever, J*

Lydia read and re-read those few words at least a dozen times. She scrambled for her poetry anthology and found the poem. It was "First Love" by John Clare. She read it, and re-read it savouring every word. To think he had sent such a lovely poem. But best of all were his own words `Always and Forever`. Oh, how could she have ever doubted Jack`s motives? What must he have thought of her behaviour this morning? She could have given everything away, destroyed everything. He called her his Lady, she must act like one.

"Your mam wants you downstairs Miss," Polly called, bringing her back to earth with a bump and a sigh. Ah, well, being busy would keep her mind occupied. Meanwhile, she had a secret, a delicious, wonderful secret, and she would keep it hidden away like her poem from Jack until the Ball.

The following day was another cloudless sunny Sunday. She pinned on her straw hat, but frowned at her reflection in the mirror. Her mother may have altered the old rose-bud dress to fit her, but still made her feel like an overgrown schoolgirl. But no matter, she reasoned. She would play the part – be calm and composed.

Just as she was leading the children through the lych-gate, they all stopped in their tracks.

"Ooh, Miss what's that `orrible noise?" wailed little Georgie.

The source of the terrible honking was coming from a grand open-topped motor car, as it edged its way past the church. At the wheel sat Edwin Bengeworth, his father beside him. His mother and two sisters were in the back, the youngest girl, Margaret sitting on her mother's lap. They acknowledged the gaping onlookers with an occasional regal wave. Lydia and the children were in time to form a guard of honour for the party as they trooped grandly through the lych-gate. Both the Squire and Edwin raised their hats to Lydia, and she could have sworn that Edwin winked.

As she mouthed the words to "Let us with a Gladsome Mind" in church, and the Reverend Peabody intoned his thankfully brief sermon, her mind wandered time and again to Jack. She recited his poem over and over in her head and re-lived the magical moments in the rain. She closed her eyes and felt his hands on her body, and a warm glow spread to her face. Her eyes snapped open and she looked guiltily around her. How could she have such thoughts, harbour her secret longings in the house of God? The chid next to her dropped her hymn book and Lydia was glad of the diversion of picking it up.

Outside church, she chatted to Lizzie as she waited with the children.

"My word Harriet Bengeworth looks a picture!" Lizzie exclaimed following Lydia`s gaze as she watched the Squire and his family walk towards the car.

Harriet held on to her wide-brimmed hat trimmed with pastel pink and blue roses which matched her diaphanous dress. Lydia felt like a parlour maid in comparison. How could she ever hope to look as stylish and graceful?

She joined her parents to walk home, and as they drew level with the motor car, Edwin, looking very red in the face was turning the starting handle. A tremendous roar suddenly emanated from under the machine, and Edwin smiled in triumph. He raised his hat to the Winters.

"Pity about the tennis party. Come next week. I`ll pick you up in the car. It`s a Bugatti. Isn`t she a beauty?" Lydia lowered her eyes and blushed.

"I`m afraid my brother and his friend have left for a walking holiday in the North."

"But you can play, can`t you?" Edwin now sounded as if he was talking to a retarded child.

"I`m sorry Lydia will be busy next weekend. But I am sure she is grateful for the invitation." It was her father who came to her rescue.

"Dashed bad luck. Never mind then. I do hope you'll come to the Ball. Won't be too busy then, I hope." He smoothed his moustache and arched an eyebrow.

"No indeed, we are all looking forward to it enormously." Lydia kept her face expressionless. What was it about Edwin Bengeworth? He fascinated and repelled her at the same time.

"Very well then. We'll bid you good-day." Edwin got into the car, honked the horn, and roared with laughter, and the car moved forward in two frantic lurches, then sped gracefully on up the hill.

"Thank you father." Lydia said.

"Eh,what? Couldn't have you going there without a chaperon. Gentry he may be, but I don't like the gleam in the fellow's eye. Come along, ladies. A light lunch I think, and then what about a trip to Barbourne Park? "

It was one of her father's mellow days, and the three of them enjoyed a pleasant afternoon walking round park beside the brook. Later, they sat beneath the shade of an enormous beech and listened to the small brass band positioned in the middle of the pretty lake. In future less happy times, this would be a memory Lydia would treasure.

After supper, the following evening Henry told Eliza and Lydia about the assassination of the Archduke Ferdinand and his wife in Sarajevo, the day before. He had read about it in the Herald on the lunch time, and had obviously been pondering on it the rest of the day.

"It`s a terrible thing, Henry, but how does the fate of Austria and Hungary affect England?" asked Eliza.

"My dear, the House of Habsburg has been holding on by a thread for years. The Austro-Hungarian Empire is a mass of different races and cultures; a veritable powder keg, and Serbia has been stirring up trouble, wanting to merge with the Slav states, for some time. I suspect there will be war."

"But only a little war….um… over there, Papa, surely," ventured Lydia.

"Hmph!" Henry gave her one of his stares over his glasses. "No member of the European monarchy sneezes without a neighbouring cousin catching cold! Serbian interests will be supported by the Russian Tsar, and the Austrian Emperor will look to the Kaiser for support. I fear a stone has been thrown into a festering cess-pit and the ripples will flow out far and wide." Henry stood up, put the folded newspaper under his arm and headed for the parlour, murmuring; "Yes, far and wide, far and wide."

Lydia had heard her father making pronouncements on political matters before. Pronouncements they always were, he brooked no discussion.

As she helped her mother with the dishes, Eliza said "You know, we shall have to take a trip to town and purchase some material to make you a new summer dress."

"Oh, yes ma, and I can afford to pay for it myself now."

"Yes you can, so I`ll buy the material for the other dress. The one for the ball."

"Of course, the ball! Can it be in the latest style, something like Harriet Bengeworth was wearing at church yesterday, for instance?"

"Mmmm. Like Harriet Bengeworth indeed?" Eliza laughed. "We shall find a pattern, and you shall have the latest style. Everyone will think you have been fitted out by the best Parisian couturiers!"

Lydia hugged her mother and planted a huge kiss on her cheek. "Oh, thank you, ma! You're the best mother in the world!"

Unknown to her mother, with Polly's help she had been learning to pile her hair in a more sophisticated fashion on top of her head, teasing and twisting the strands to look like styles she had seen in The Lady magazine, copies of which Polly's sister – who worked at the Grange - had been given by Harriet Bengeworth. She would cut out pictures of the latest style dresses to show her mother and persuade her to make it. She was determined to look her very best for the Squire's Ball; to be beautiful for Jack; to make him proud of her. She had so much to look forward to!

She wrote about her plans for the dress in her journal, and before she closed it, she read the entry she had made Saturday night.

Darling Jack has declared his love for me, and I for him. It shall be our Secret until he can speak to his father. I have never kept a secret before, but the keeping of this secret, I now know, shall be my strength, for it is a good and loving secret.

She had pasted an envelope in the back cover of the book, and in it she placed Jack`s pillow poem.

Tonight, once more, she closed her eyes clutching his pillow case. When she had returned from the station two days ago she had felt like falling to pieces, but as she breathed in his scent which still clung to the linen in her hands, she felt calmer and full of hope. She had so much to look forward to; nothing could possibly go wrong now.

Ten

"Come along, boys! Change of plan - your chariot awaits!"

Alfred and Jack stared at the vision before them – Ada dressed in knickerbockers and riding boots, legs astride, hands on hips. The boys were packed, ready to go waiting in the Palace foyer for a taxi to be summoned to take them to the station.

With a flick of her wrist and a quick word, Ada dispatched the porters to carry out their luggage. "Close your mouth Alfred. I`m taking you to Cumberland, and I may even stay a day or two! Emily can`t come, I`m afraid, but she sends her regards."

In no time at all they were leaving the crowded streets of Manchester behind. Alfred admired the green countryside around them lounging in the back seat of the Daimler, as Ada and Jack chatted about family matters.

"And your charming family Alfred?" Ada jolted him out of his reverie. "They must be so proud of you; such an interesting family. Mmmm. They have definitely left an impression on my cousin. Particularly your sister." She shot a glance at Jack sitting next to her.

"Pity Emily couldn't have joined us," Jack said in an effort to change the subject

"Yes, poor Emily, but she must never over do things." Ada turned to Alfred. "But you boys have been so good for her! I haven`t seen her so lively in months. You must keep your word and write, Alfred.

She'd love that. I must bring her to visit you in Claines."

"Well, of…of course…" Alfred spluttered.

Ada laughed like a drain. "I can see what you're thinking! Whatever would Claines make of me! Don't worry dear, I'll come in disguise!" She roared with laughter again, and Alfred was not quite sure if she was serious. What an extraordinary woman Ada was! He felt sure that like Jack she was no snob, but it was a fact of life that their family backgrounds and class were miles apart. As he fingered the leather upholstery he still found it hard to believe he was part of their lives at this particular moment in time.

Soon Ada started singing, everything from musical hall songs to the Hallelujah Chorus, the boys joining in when they knew the words.

They arrived at a grand Victorian house owned by friends of Jack's family who themselves were abroad. The staff and the house, which had a commanding view of Lake Windermere, were at their disposal, and as they knew all the neighbouring landowners they would have the right to roam the hills as they pleased. Once again Alfred marvelled at his friend's gilded lifestyle. The rain had stopped and they were soon chugging across the lake in a small steamboat as the setting sun heralded a fine day ahead.

"I say!" said Alfred picking up the newspaper the following day. "Who's the Archduke Ferdinand?"

Ada's head shot up immediately. "Why? What's happened to him?"

"He's been assassinated in Sarajevo. Seems he's heir to the Austro-Hungarian Empire."

"Yes indeed. That's a powder keg waiting to explode. If they declare war on Serbia, the Kaiser will be polishing his helmet."

The boys looked at her questioningly. "Well you must know the man is unstable, always spoiling for a fight. Let's just hope he won't need to polish his sabre to vent his fury!" and she roared with laughter. They went in to breakfast, all thoughts of sabres and wars totally forgotten.

The weather was glorious and Ada stayed with them, walking the fells, singing as they went. She even took photographs with a huge, cumbersome camera on one occasion. When she returned to Manchester for a Red Cross Meeting two days later, the boys missed her cheery company, but soon fell into a routine of walking, talking and enjoying the glorious scenery. Jack's only regret was that Lydia was not there to share it. But he wrote to her, telling her of their diversion to Manchester, of Ada and Emily. He waxed lyrical about the overwhelming beauty of Windermere, Grasmere and Rydal Water, and told her he felt sure she would share it with him one day in the future.

Yes, he reflected, he was indeed beginning to live with Lydia in his heart. He couldn't erase her memory any easier than he could stop breathing; she was everywhere.

On their last morning as he watched Alfred packing away his clothes and maps – for he had meticulously planned their walks, Jack was dreading going home to Leamington, for he would have to spend time at his father's firm, and he knew deep down he would never be a lawyer, yet he had no burning ambition to be anything else.

"Time to go home, Alfred. I shall be the dutiful son, and bore myself rigid clerking for a few weeks. I shall of course have to catch up on the social rounds which no doubt Mother will have all neatly planned out for me." Jack sighed heavily and looked at his friend. "I shall miss you, old chap. I would ask you to come, but you'd hate it."

Alfred nodded sagely, thinking that he might not enjoy the socialising, but he would actually give his right arm to work inside a solicitor's office.

"You haven't forgotten the Summer Ball at The Grange have you?" he asked.

"Of course not. I shall come the day before. At present it is the only light on my horizon. Three more weeks, then I shall see dear Lydia again."

"Jack, please tread carefully with her," entreated Alfred.

"Alfred, that is what I was leading up to. I shall play the dutiful son at home, and then I shall tell my parents of my intentions. I shall finish college, then I mean to marry Lydia. When I come to the ball, I shall speak to your father, and escort her to the ball as her suitor."

"And you think it will be that easy? They will consent, just like that, to you marrying the daughter of a village schoolmaster?"

"Why not? Once they meet her, they will see how beautiful and accomplished she is. I know they probably have some minor heiress lined up for me, but hell, the family is rolling in money, it's not as if we need a marriage of convenience."

81

Alfred knew that Jack was not really that naive. Lydia may be beautiful and accomplished, but she was like an untamed filly next to the groomed thoroughbreds of upper class society even he had been privy to encounter.

Jack seemed to read his thoughts. "I know what you`re thinking. But it wouldn`t be the first time such matches have been made. We are living in the twentieth century. I`ll talk them round, you`ll see." He downed the rest of his brandy. "I have to. I love her."

*

Just before they left for the station the following morning, Jack received a letter from Lydia.

She told him she willed her spirit to be there with him in that beautiful place he described so well. She said the harvest had started, and she looked forward to joining in at the weekends. Most of all she was looking forward to the ball. Her ma had bought her yards of silk and lace, and together they were going to make her a beautiful gown. "You shall not know the colour until the day. Oh, Jack I love you so." She had enclosed words from Christina Rosetti;

"Love me, for I love you – and answer me,
Love me, for I love you – so shall we stand
As happy equals in the flowering land
Of love, that knows not a dividing sea."

Jack sighed and placed it carefully in his inside pocket next to his heart.

The two boys parted later in Birmingham to go their separate ways, but their holiday had forged a deeper bond between them which would be there, always and forever.

Alfred too reflected on the holiday and his fondness for Jack, but it was Emily`s pale, sad face haunted his dreams. They had exchanged letters and she had expressed a hope that they would meet again. Perhaps he could visit Nice in the Autumn or Spring?

He sighed deeply. Nice in the Autumn or Spring! How could that be possible? He must content himself with a pen-friendship, anything more would be reaching for the stars. Like Lydia and Jack. Oh, he hoped that something would come of their dreams, but somehow he felt that`s what they were. Dreams.

*

Back at school house, where he had been greeted with great warmth, Alfred noticed the change in Lydia. She seemed so composed. Was she growing up at last? After supper, they walked down to the swing, and Alfred gave her Jack`s message.

"He sends his love, and says he can`t wait for the ball." For some reason he omitted to say he would escort her. Lydia blushed; she was glad of the twilight.

"It`s alright. I know." Alfred said, turning away from her.

"Know what?" she whispered.

"I know you love each other. But don`t worry, I shan`t say anything."

"I so envied you, Alfred, being with Jack every day. Walking round that beautiful countryside, sharing everything with him." She sat on the swing, hugging the one rope and staring into the distance. It was getting dark, yet she seemed to look luminous in her pale pink country frock. In the moonlight Alfred got a sudden sense of her vulnerability.

He stood at the side of the swing and held the other rope. "Don`t hope for too much, sis."

"What do you mean? You sound like Ma. Jack loves me, I love him. You said you know that." Her voice rang out in the silent garden.

"Ssshhh. Ma and Pa will hear!"

Lydia jumped off the swing.

"Oh, that would never do, would it? You can be his friend, but I can never be his lover! Are you jealous, dear brother, jealous because you don`t know what it`s like to be in love?"

"Lydia! Don`t say such foolish things!" Alfred followed her as she strode off further down the garden.

"Foolish am I? Oh, yes, of course. Silly, childish, headstrong Lydia! Well, big brother, if only you knew!" Lydia faced him with her hands on her hips.

Alfred said quietly, "I think I do." And started to walk away.

"What, what do you think you know?" Lydia held his arm to stop him walking away.

He turned and held his sister`s shoulders. He kept his voice low and calm. "I do understand, Lyddy. You`re wrong, I do know what it`s like to…to…fall for somebody. But like you, it can never be. We`re out of our depth Lydia! It would be best if you forgot about Jack. You would have to, if it wasn`t for this damned ball!"

"What do you mean?" Lydia was nearly sobbing now. "I`m looking forward so much to the ball, we all are! Jack is looking forward to it, ma is making me a dress, it will be so special…Oh Alfred, I`m sorry if you have been disappointed in love, but surely you want me to be happy? Jack says if we`re patient, we can be together."

"Maybe you will, little sis. Maybe you will. Now dry your eyes. For heaven`s sake don`t let ma and pa see something`s up. There`s three weeks to go, and I`m sure the ball will be everything you dream it will be."

*

That night, Lydia buried her face in Jack`s pillow as she did every night. His scent had faded away now, but it was something of his, something that made him feel near. By the light of her candle, she read and re-read his poems and letters. She smoothed them and kissed them and re-tied them in her blue ribbons and placed them in her rosewood jewellery box, one of the few items in her possession which had any value.

She still wrote in her journal, and of late her jottings had been mostly about the mundane tasks of her daily existence. She didn`t used to think of her life as mundane, but everything now was mundane without Jack. Tonight she wrote;

`How good it was to have Alfred home! Oh, the Lakes sound wonderful; even my unimaginative brother was moved by the beauty of it all. But Jack made it come alive for me. Please God I shall see them one day with Jack.

85

It seems that Alfred has experienced unrequited love. I am quite astonished! Perhaps that is why he was so pessimistic about Jack and me being together.

But we shall be! Please God, we shall be!

Oh, I can`t wait for the ball!`

Eleven

Jack had spent a miserable couple of weeks in Leamington. As he sat on the train to Worcester on the morning of the Squire's ball, he felt he never wanted to go home again. Home! That cold, ordered, austere house which held no comfort or respite for him in any sense. He had only seen his mother at dinner in the evening, and she seemed more frigid and remote than ever. He found he had nothing in common with his haughty brother, and his little sister had seemed like a frightened little rabbit.

He had been quite happy to escape to his father's solicitor's practice during most days on the pretext of work, but had been bored and disinterested most of the time. He smiled when he recalled teasing the frigid old secretary Miss Harcourt, whom he had christened Miss Hardboard. She had been outraged to find him using her typewriter to write to Lydia, but when he left her a snippet from a sonnet on another occasion, she had softened a little towards him, and they even talked about their favourite poems. She had even blushed a little when he presented her with a rose he had stolen from the garden at home, before he left.

Try as he may though, he had never been able to win his mother round with any of his charm. She had looked at him with scorn when he had tried to talk about his friend Alfred - the sojourn at his home, and his walking holiday.

"You must be so relieved to be back with your own kind," she had said.

But worst of all had been his talk with his father. As he watched the green fields of Warwickshire roll by, he shuddered as he relived that awful evening two days before when his father had returned from Westminster.

They had retired after dinner to drink brandy and smoke, and Jack felt relieved to be away from the tense atmosphere of the dining room. He waffled on about some of his adventures at Oxford.

"Mmm. Time of your life, m`boy, time of your life. Don`t expect you to get a first or anything, but," he had paused to exhale a cloud of smoke, "Don`t let me down, boy. I hope to hear of better results next year."

Jack had shifted uncomfortably in his seat. "I am trying Father, really I am. Next year I`ll buckle down, I promise. I am trying to be useful at the office, but I feel I`m getting in peoples` way, really."

"Mmm I`ll have a word. Mind you, off to Worcester again soon aren`t you? You seem quite taken with your friend and his family. A curious attachment it seems to me."

It was now or never, thought Jack. "Alfred is really a splendid fellow, father. You would approve of him. He seems to bring out the best in me. He has had to work so very hard to be where he is, and he`s made me see the virtue and necessity of applying oneself to study." He saw his father consider this.

"In fact," Jack stumbled on, "in quite a short time, I have become fond of all the family. He has a sister, Lydia, and she is a beautiful, accomplished young lady."

"Oh yes? And how old is Lydia?"

"Eighteen. She is a teacher in her father`s school. She is pretty and intelligent – did I say she loves poetry? – she sings in the local choir, and…"

"And you seem to be besotted with her."

"Father, I am in love with her." There! He had said it. Jack sat upright and waited for the disapproving tirade.

Francis took a sip of his brandy, and tapped the ash of his cigar into the huge cut-glass ashtray at his elbow. He shrugged. "You`ll probably fall in love many times before you marry. Lydia will just be one of many, before you marry some-one of your own class."

"Lydia is the girl for me, father. I would like your permission to speak to her father." Jack felt the blood rush to his face. He gulped down his brandy.

"You have a university degree to obtain, and years of pupillage before you can consider marriage." A hint of impatience was now creeping into Francis` tone.

"But I can still do all that! We are quite happy to wait a few years..."

"We!" Francis stubbed out his cigar and stood up. "There is no `we`! I suggest you forget all about this ... this Lydia, and her wretched family. Keep Alfred as a friend if you must, but leave it at that. I forbid you to see her again!"

Jack stood up. "But father, I have accepted an invitation to a ball next weekend which is being held by the local Squire, Sir Frederick Bengeworth. All Alfred`s family are attending; I promised."

Francis walked towards his son, and put an arm around his shoulder. "Alright, go to the ball, fulfil your obligations. But let her brother be her escort. Enjoy yourself with this young lady, by all means" he winked salaciously "get her out of your system. You will y`know. You don`t see it now, but believe me, in a few years you`ll see I was right."

Jack bit his lip and fought for self-control.

"I`m glad we`ve had this opportunity to talk, son. It`s been a long time." It was a warm summer evening, and Francis led him onto the terrace, draining his brandy glass. "It may also be some time before we talk again. I`m going back to London tomorrow. We`re on the brink of a war, Jack. I see no way of stopping it."

Jack was speechless – his head was still reeling from his father`s dismissal of Lydia.

"Yes. There are those of us who believe that Britain should keep out of an essentially European conflict; the Austrian-Hungarian and German alliance against France and Russia. All stirred up by the Arch-Duke`s assassination in Serbia, don`t y`know. It`s been simmering for years. Looks like we`ll come in to support Belgium, France and Russia. But don`t worry son, whatever happens, it`ll probably all be over by Christmas." He put his arm around Jack once more – he had never known his father be so tactile. "So you see, there are always greater matters of importance than our own whims. I want to be able to get on with my responsibilities knowing that everyone here is getting on with theirs." He slapped him on the back and Jack`s heart sank as he watched his father walk through the drawing room, pausing only to put his brandy glass down on a side table.

The lurch of the train as it drew into Foregate Street Station brought Jack back to the present. Whatever happened, he would give Lydia her night at the ball – and then? Well, there simply had to be a way.

At School House, as the family greeted him their eyes met, and Jack felt the familiar lurch in his heart as Lydia looked at him, her sweet face so full of love and expectation.

He managed to take Alfred aside and explain his father's refusal. Alfred had been quiet and circumspect – it had not really surprised him. They both agreed to concentrate on making Lydia's night at the ball a night to remember – she was so excited. It was an important event for all the family. It signified elevation into the best social sphere in the County for the Winters.

Later, whilst dressing, Jack heard the loud honking of a car horn. He rushed downstairs as Eliza opened the door to Ada, resplendent in tweed knickerbockers and yellow blouse.

"Oh, there you are Jack! Been to Birmingham for a Red Cross Convention, and thought I'd look you up. Your mama told me you were here, sorry I missed you this morning, but then I thought; why not drive over to Worcester? And here I am! But I see you're going somewhere."

Jack introduced her to Eliza and Lydia who had appeared in the hallway with an astonished looking Polly peering over her shoulder.

"We're going to our neighbour's Grand Summer Ball. Perhaps you noticed the house on the hill?" Eliza began to explain.

"Why, how absolutely thrilling! I'll tootle off. But I see Jack is practically ready!"

"Yes, well, we thought we'd go to the pub and leave the ladies to it..."

"What a splendid idea. Come on then, I'll join you, then I'll make my way into town and find a hotel. I say, how are you getting there? Do you have a carriage?"

"Dr. Morton, a neighbour is transporting us," Eliza said proudly.

"Jolly good. But if I can be of any help with transport... would the youngsters like me to take them in the car?" Ada looked from Alfred to Lydia, to Jack.

"Ooh, thank you. That would be lovely!" chirped Lydia.

"That's agreed then. Come on Jack, I'm absolutely parched. Let's see this famous Inn in a churchyard. Toodle pip!"

"Who the devil is that?" Henry exclaimed as he walked into the hall.

"It's Jack's cousin, Ada Chellingworth," said Lydia. "She's got that amazing motor car, and she's going to take us to the ball!"

"Amazing is the word, Lydia. Whatever next?"

"Come along, Father, we'll join them at The Mug while the ladies dress," Alfred piped up.

"What? That woman is going into the Mug?"

"She's a Suffragette, father." Alfred said and Henry nodded sagely as if it explained everything.

"In about an hour, ladies?" Alfred said.

Lydia's dress was of cornflower blue silk, and very much of the latest style; high-waisted with short sleeves. The neckline was scooped, revealing a modest décolletage, and Lydia wore nothing at her neck. Her fair hair had been teased and looped high on her head, and had caused Polly much consternation, as she had painstakingly threaded seed pearls between the curls. She wore a pair of Eliza's drop pearl earrings, and more seed pearls had been sewn into the bodice. The skirt looked deceptively straight, but at the back there was more fullness, which would enable Lydia to dance without encumbrance. She wore a white velvet cape over her shoulders and elbow-length white gloves.

Alfred escorted her to the car, where Jack waited, holding his breath. Lydia looked beautiful. His Lydia, the girl he wanted for his wife, the girl his father had forbidden him to marry. He felt his heart was breaking, and soon, he would have to break hers. He took her hand, kissed it, and looking into her eyes said; "Well! I thought we were taking Lydia Winters to the Ball, who can this ravishing impostor be?"

Oh, Jack! My handsome, lovely Jack! Lydia was almost overwhelmed with happiness, but she smiled demurely and climbed into the back of the Daimler, where Alfred joined her. Jack climbed in the front with Ada. A frisson of disappointment fluttered in Lydia's breast. Her brother was escorting her.

"You'll have all the young beaux of the neighbourhood falling at your feet young lady. Jack is right, you look beautiful Lydia. You must be so proud of your sister, Alfred."

Her brother grinned like the cat that had eaten all the cream. "I am indeed, Ada." He squeezed Lydia's hand to reassure her.

Lydia smiled at her brother then stared at Jack's back. This was always going to be the night of her life, but how could it be without Jack at her side?

Twelve

They crunched to a halt in front of the Grange, the car and its occupants attracting admiring glances from several other guests arriving at the same time.

Alfred led Lydia up the steps, followed by Jack, where they were greeted by Sir Frederick and Lady Amelia in the hallway. They walked into the ball room – actually a large drawing room and dining room which was opened out on such occasions by folding back huge doors – and the electric light from enormous chandeliers, the colours of the dresses and the sumptuous setting, left Lydia spellbound for a moment. A quartet of musicians struck up a lively tune, and Alfred took her hand to dance.

Many of the more mature guests were seated around the edge of the panelled floor, and their parents joined the Mortons. But Lydia had no time to sit, as Will Shawcross, a friend of Alfred`s was at her elbow requesting a dance, this time a waltz. As she whirled round the room she scanned the room for Jack, but he was nowhere to be seen. He did re-appear when the dance was over, however, carrying a tray of champagne glasses. Then Lydia watched as the Rev. Peabody commandeered him and steered him towards his daughter Maude whom he accompanied for a quadrille. Lydia felt a huge pang of disappointment and couldn`t bear to look at them. She turned her back and muttered small talk with her mother.

As the band struck up a waltz she felt a hand at her elbow.

"I wonder if you have a gap on your dance card Miss Lydia,"

Edwin Bengeworth was offering his hand. He looked impeccably dashing in his evening dress, his grey eyes openly appraising her.

"Oh, I don`t have a card…." Lydia realised he was teasing, and relaxed a little.

"We`re no longer so formal, thank God. I can`t think why you haven`t been to our Balls before."

Oh can`t you? thought Lydia, but she merely smiled up at him.

"What a lovely smile you have. You`re quite the Belle of the Ball, you know."

"Am I? Oh, come, all these lovely ladies..." And as she glanced around, many of the `lovely ladies` were giving her quite hostile looks, particularly his sister, Harriet.

"…can`t hold a candle to you. You must let me escort you into dinner. Although, it is very informal, of course, a buffet. But you must allow me the pleasure…"

"Well, of course, kind Sir."

As they danced Lydia was aware that they were the centre of attention, and she revelled in it, enjoying being held in Edwin`s strong arms. "I hope Jack is watching, and what do I care?" she thought.

The dance finished, and like Moses parting the Red Sea, Edwin held Lydia`s hand aloft and swept her through to the Orangery, where amongst the rare orchids, a huge table, groaning with food was laid out. She resolved to put Jack at the back of her mind. Here was the host, the Squire`s son, making her feel like a princess, as he took a plate for her, and holding

96

it with his own, picked out the best delicacies for her. He led her out onto the terrace, where more small tables and chairs were positioned, with what was probably a commanding view over the gardens, but little could be seen beyond a few feet of the terrace on this moonless night. It was a cool evening, but Lydia welcomed it after the heat of the ballroom. He held a chair out for her, and as she sat down she felt his breath on her shoulders. She froze. Oh, why had she allowed herself to get so carried away, and where was Jack? A waiter materialised with more champagne, and as more guests drifted onto the terrace, Lydia began to put her misgivings to the back of her mind. What could happen with all these people here?

Another young couple joined them, they prattled on about their recent visit to Paris. Lydia listened graciously, nodding as she thought appropriate.

"...And your gown", the girl, Kate, was addressing her. "Lydia, did you say? Was your gown from a Parisian Fashion House? I must say it`s most unusual, quite charming in its simple way."

Lydia sensed she was patronising her. "Oh, no. I have never been to Paris. My dear Mama made it for me. We purchased the gloves from Fownes, however. I do think it`s terribly important to support our local industries, don`t you? Oh, there`s my dear Mama now. You will excuse me."

The group sat open-mouthed as she swept past them. Then Edwin burst out laughing. "I say, isn`t she superb? Simply wonderful!"

Lydia was looking for Jack again, but instead found her parents in the large hallway, where Henry motioned for her to sit down.

"Damned way of eating! Little better than a picnic. Now, young lady, I think you had better calm down a bit. You'll soon be dancing with every young buck here. A little decorum would not go amiss for the rest of the evening."

"Nonsense!" said Eliza. "There is nothing improper about Lydia's behaviour, Henry. Your daughter looks quite a beauty tonight, and it's only natural that Mr. Edwin would want to dance with her. Don't be an old curmudgeon!"

Alfred diffused the tension by taking her to speak to Will and his sister Lottie.

She had just accepted Will's offer to dance again, when Edwin Bengeworth resurfaced between them, and took her hand.

"Awfully bad form, I know, old chap, but it's my ball, y'know."

Lydia smiled graciously. He was right; it was his ball, and she felt very flattered that he seemed to be constantly seeking her out. It was only a dance. But where, oh where was Jack?

It was the St. Bernard's waltz, which meant that the male dancer passed on the female partner to the next male after every sequence, and Edwin scowled as he watched her twirl away. Lydia was enjoying herself, basking in the attention and enjoying the music, when suddenly she came face to face with Jack. She felt a mixture of relief and anger, but he merely grinned and held her tightly. When he should have passed her on, he whisked her outside the circle, and carried on waltzing. When they reached the door, he led her out onto the terrace. They were alone, as the other guests had either re-joined the dancers or found it too chilly.

"I was enjoying the dance. Why have you brought me out here?"

"I couldn't let you go once I had you." Their eyes locked, but Jack tore himself away and went to one of the tables and picked up two glasses of champagne. He handed one to Lydia, and clinked her glass.

"Here's to the Belle of the Ball, to Lady Lydia," he said, and as he drained the glass in one gulp.

She put her glass down. "Let's go back in Jack. Don't get drunk and spoil it. Come and dance with me again. It's wonderful, I've never known anything like it!"

"Oh, so this is what you want from life is it? Well let me tell you I've been to more parties and balls like this than you've had hot dinners. Quite honestly, they bore me to tears."

"Well, aren't you the lucky one? Well, silly me, of course you are. The lucky and privileged Jack Albright. Bored to tears are you? Then I'm most surprised you turned up tonight. You certainly didn't keep your promise to escort me, what other promises have you broken, Jack?"

They stood looking at each other in the still night air, and Jack felt his colour rise.

Lydia swallowed the lump in her throat. His silence seemed to say everything. He would not be speaking to her father, after all. It was all over.

Without a word she turned to go. He grabbed her hand.

"Don`t go. Don`t go back in and dance with him."

Lydia shook her hand free and stepped back. "Don`t tell me you`re jealous, Jack! Fancy that! Well, let me tell you, that I shall dance with whom I please. Edwin has been most attentive, which is more than I can say for you."

Jack stepped in front of the door and barred her way. "Then dance with me. Please don`t go like this."

"What`s the matter with you? You don`t own me, far from it! I will not allow one mistake to ruin my life." She looked past him, and could see a group of people looking towards them, concerned by the raised voices.

"Let me pass!" Lydia said through clenched teeth.

"Only if you`ll go in with me!" Jack muttered back.

"I`d rather dance with the Kaiser!" she shouted, and ran along the terrace and down the steps onto the lawn. She had intended to run round the house and enter it by another way, but once there, her heeled shoes sank into the soft turf, so on instinct she kicked them off. She found the cool grass comforting. Leaving her shoes, she picked up her skirt and ran into the darkness away from the house, and didn`t stop until she was aware of the faint outline of some sort of structure. She felt round the stone pillars, and realised it was some sort of folly or perhaps a summer house, but there were no walls. Her eyes were now accustomed to the dark, and she found a stone bench along one side. She sat down, and getting her breath back she looked across a dark expanse to the house. Every room seemed to be brightly lit, and she could even see figures moving about downstairs. Movement in the nearby shrubbery made her jump, then she heard Jack softly calling her name. Within seconds he was there beside her.

"How did you find me, it`s so dark?" she whispered.

"Of course I found you. We`re kindred spirits, you and I. My beautiful Lady Lydia." He reached out and held her in his arms. All her anger had dissipated; she just knew she was where she wanted to be, as his lips found hers.

On the terrace, Edwin Bengeworth stared into the night. He lit a cigar and as he blew out the smoke, he raised an eyebrow. He had witnessed the quarrel between Jack and Lydia, and knew they were out there somewhere, probably in The Folly. He guessed at what might be happening, and envied Jack Albright.

Well, he mused, she may be damaged goods, but he wanted her all the same. And what Edwin Bengeworth wanted, he usually got.

Lydia was never to know it, but it was thanks to the `silly empty headed` young lady called Kate, whom she had met earlier on that evening, that her intimacy with Jack would remain a secret. After their unplanned tryst in the folly, Jack and Lydia made their way back to the house, at first wrapped in each other`s arms, aware only of each other, and blessing the cover of darkness.

Jack stroked Lydia`s tear-stained cheek. "I`m so sorry, my darling. I begged my father to see my point of view, but it was hopeless. I had to come back today, I had to keep part of my promise."

"I half-guessed when you didn't escort me. I just wouldn't let myself believe it."

"You looked so ravishing, so beautiful. I just wanted tonight to be perfect for you, but as ever, I let you down. After the dance with Maude Peabody, I just watched you from afar. You could have the world at your feet, you know, little lady."

"I just want you, Jack Albright."

"I'll find a way. I have to find a way, and I will I promise. Tonight has taught me that much, I can't live without you, and I can't wait for years and years." He kissed her fingertips. "But we must go back, you'll be missed."

They walked back to the house, but as they neared the pool of light beneath the terrace, Lydia gasped at the state of her creased gown, dishevelled hair, and wet feet.

"Never mind, I've got an idea," laughed Jack. "Hitch up your skirt, and I'll give you a piggy back".

Lydia duly obliged, and whooping at the top of his voice, Jack ran with her towards the terrace, where he fell over, and both of them rolled on the damp grass, screaming with laughter. Kate and her young man, Horace had wandered onto the terrace to cool down from the dancing. Kate was quite taken with the spectacle.

"Oooh, Horace! What fun! Come on, you can give me a piggy back too!" She grabbed her companion and led him down to the steps, abandoning her shoes next to Lydia's. The commotion soon attracted others, and within minutes several young couples, fuelled with champagne and the adrenalin from dancing, were racing across the lawn; the young men acting as noble steeds (or donkeys) driven by laughing young ladies in various stages of hysteria. In turn they attracted a large audience of the older guests, who cheered them on - everyone finding the whole affair hilarious. Except of course for Henry, who shouted for Lydia to stop at once.

Sir Frederick took his arm sympathetically. "I shouldn't worry, sir. It's only high spirits! It's probably all that champagne."

"Hmmph! That's as maybe, but look at them! I've never seen anything like it!"

"Oh, dear me! Were you never young once? It all looks pretty harmless to me. Leave them be, man. Let them have their fun while they can. Who knows what tomorrow may bring?"

Henry nodded and coughed self-consciously, and let Eliza lead him back into the orangery, where they waited for the Mortons, who seemed to be as entertained by the 'races' as everyone else.

Lydia and Jack re-joined the guests looking every bit as flushed, damp and unkempt as most of the other young couples. Alfred had not joined the melee but had cheered them on. They found Lydia's cape, amid much back-slapping and laughter – and a very civil farewell from the Squire and his wife. The party was over. Edwin may have felt that they had stolen his thunder, but he was gracious enough not to show it, particularly as most of his departing friends were congratulating him on a night to remember.

He bowed graciously to Lydia and shook Jack's hand. Their eyes locked for a second, and Jack was left in no doubt that he had a formidable opponent. But tonight was his – he slapped Edwin on the shoulder, and ran down the steps with Lydia, who was still carrying her shoes. They were amazed to see Ada waiting for them.

"Get in, then! My God, what have you two been up to? You look a frightful mess!" she said.

"We`ve been having piggy back races!" said Lydia, still flushed with excitement.

Jack and Lydia sat together in the back, sinking back into the seat and against each other, their hands entwined.

Mmmm, thought Ada. And that`s not all you`ve been up to. Looks like you`ve had quite a wild night, my beauties. But where can it all lead, I wonder?

Thirteen

Lydia turned over in her little bed and stretched luxuriantly, reliving the memory of last night in Jack's arms. Oh, why had she doubted him? Jack said she had to trust him. They would have to wait; it would test their love and fidelity, he had said. For now, there could be no more episodes like last night, or stolen kisses. So be it, she resolved. She would prove to Jack that she could be patient. An image of the Lady of Shalott popped into her head. "Mmmm. I certainly won't be shutting myself off from the world though. No gilded cage for me," she murmured sitting up in bed, hoping she hadn't overslept. Then she saw it - her crumpled blue dress lying on a heap in the floor.

"Oh, my dress, my lovely dress!" She dressed quickly, scooped up the garment and tip-toed downstairs to the wash house and walked straight into Polly.

"Oh, dear Miss Lydia! Now what have you been up to? Not summat else you want me to sort out? And 'ere's me with Master Jack's shirt and trousers from your last adventure." She lifted the hem, inspected the soiled dress and tutted.

"Now it wasn't raining last night – to the best of my knowledge. But looks like you was rollin' about on the grass again, and gawd knows what else!"

"For heaven's sake stop tutting Polly! Yes, I did tumble on the grass, and so did Master Jack … And don't look like that! So did half of the young couples there last night!"

"What were it then, Miss? One of them there orgies?"

"Orgies? Whatever can you mean?" Lydia was genuinely confused, then seeing Polly giggle, the penny dropped.

"Polly! We were all tumbling on the grass because we had piggyback races. It was tremendous fun!"

"I see. Um, but then again I don`t. I en`t `ad a piggy back race since I was six, but then again, them nobs gets up to all sorts so I `eard."

"My dress, Polly!"

"Give it `ere. I`ll try tamping with a bit o` glycerine, then soap and water on them grass stains."

"Oh, Polly you`re an angel!"

"More than can be said for you," Polly muttered under her breath. "Good party was it then?" she said aloud.

"Oh, it was heavenly, and grand, and … like nothing I`ve ever seen! Polly, do you know they have huge chandeliers, lit by electric lights!"

"Yes Miss. You know me sister works there. No doubt I`ll `ear all about it when she comes `ome on her day off." She laid the dress on the table. "And Master Jack? Did you dance with him?"

"Of course! I had many partners as it happens. Edwin Bengeworth himself danced with me, and chose the food for me. He looked rather put out when Jack danced with me."

Polly looked appalled. "You give `im a wide berth Miss. He`s a right `un. The Squire don`t employ no pretty wenches any more, `cos he`s been such a devil in the past."

106

"What about your sister?" asked Lydia, horrified.

"She`s alright. `elps as her`s got buck teeth and warts!"

They both giggled, and for a minute it was like ten year old girls again.

*

Ada called at School House after Sunday lunch. Henry and Eliza didn`t know quite what to make of this fearsome cousin of Jack`s, but just like her nephew she sat among them as if this was how she spent every Sunday afternoon. Everyone began to relax as she was soon entertaining them with her stories of some of the characters she encountered in her different roles in the community. Later, Henry and Eliza were happy to doze away the afternoon as Lydia and Alfred took their guests on a stroll to Bevere, a local beauty spot.

As they strolled slowly beneath the wonderful avenue of chestnut trees leading towards the river, Ada held Jack back.

"You must know that you are playing with fire, Jack." Ada launched into the subject straight away. "And don`t feign surprise. You know exactly what I am talking about. You have a position in society. Your father has great expectations of you. You must not toy with Lydia`s affections."

Jack stopped in his tracks. "Toy? For God`s sake, I know she is no plaything! I should have walked away from here weeks ago, before… but I didn`t, and now it`s far too late for that. I am committed to Lydia."

"You are committed to your family!"

107

"Hmm. I might have guessed there was an ulterior motive to your visiting me in this humble neck of the woods."

"I am full of respect for this family Jack, and I think Lydia is delightful. But you have a duty, Jack and you know it."

"I also have a duty to Lydia. I don`t want to argue with you, Ada. Somehow I had expected you of all people to be more understanding."

"I do understand, but I also understand your father. I don`t think he will compromise on this. Ultimately you could be disinherited."

"Then so be it! We`ll elope! I`ll go and work for your brothers in the mills! In fact I was going to broach the subject with you anyway. I can`t stand the thought of more university, and I`ll never make a lawyer Ada. We`ll come to Manchester. I`m not afraid to get my hands dirty and work hard for a living if I have to."

"Fine words, but fine words won`t buy you a home and provide for a family. Love will fly out the window, when poverty walks in the door, believe me!"

"I just know I can`t give her up. But for now I know we`ll have to wait. We won`t be the first lovers who have had to keep our secret and be patient. Lydia is with me on this."

Ada took his arm again, and they strolled on in silence for a while, until the river came into sight. They could see Alfred and Lydia waving to them in the distance.

"I had planned to take the family for a drive to the Malvern hills tomorrow to thank them for their hospitality. I shall return to Leamington in the early evening. You must come with me Jack."

"I hadn't planned to leave so soon."

"Well you must." They stopped again. "Don't you see that it is an impossible situation. It is so obvious, the attraction between you. I am convinced that the mother can see it, and Henry looks decidedly uneasy at times. If you stay you will betray yourselves. You may already be the talk of the neighbourhood after last night, and it puts the whole family in an intolerable situation. Whatever you decide to do, take time to think about it. This family deserves to be treated with respect."

"Very well. Tomorrow evening."

*

The following day was August Bank Holiday Monday. Jack and Alfred travelled to Malvern by train, and Henry, Eliza and Lydia set out with Ada in the Daimler for the same destination. They were all thrilled, and even Henry's smile could be detected beneath his luxuriant growth of beard. They seemed to fly along at a tremendous speed, but their pace became more leisurely as they drew near to the hills, for the narrower roads were busy with horse-drawn vehicles of every description, bringing people to enjoy the beauty spot.

They met the boys as arranged at the bottom of the fabled St. Anne's Well. Young lads were offering lifts on donkeys up the steep incline, but they all decided to walk; Eliza and Henry stopping frequently to catch their breath.

Henry handed Ada a metal cup with water from the well. "Reputed to have magical healing properties," he muttered. "Load of nonsense of course."

They spent a pleasant hour listening to a gypsy boy playing an accordion. People smiled and tapped their feet; children danced and clapped in the sunshine. A young girl, probably a maid on her day off, grabbed her boyfriend's hand and they danced with the children. Lydia caught Jack's eye and smiled. Ada - as usual missing nothing. She knew how they longed to throw caution to the wind and join in. She also saw Henry stiffen as he noticed the loving look between his daughter and Jack.

Lydia and the boys continued walking to pick up the path to the Beacon, where they were keen to see the toposcope. Ada departed with the parents, to take them on a circuitous trip around the hills to admire the views. They were to meet later at the grand Imperial Hotel for luncheon.

On top of the Beacon, Lydia and Alfred pointed out to Jack the surrounding three counties - Worcestershire, Herefordshire and Gloucestershire, the Shropshire hills in the distance. Then he tactfully left them in each other's arms.

"I love the hills, Lydia, and although this is different to Cumberland, it has its own beauty. After all, it inspired your very own Edward Elgar to write much of his music. Let's live here one day."

Lydia sighed. "I don't care where we live. It can be a pig-sty for all I care. Just as long as I have you."

He laughed and kissed her forehead. "My dearest love. It won't be long, I promise. We may have to prepare ourselves for a future without our parents' consent, I know our love will stand the test of time. Always and forever Lydia."

"Always and forever, Jack." Nothing else needed to be said. They held each other for as long as they dared, and wished for time to stand still, but the world kept on turning.

Back home at Claines, Lydia asked about the car, so Ada lifted the bonnet for her to see the engine. "Would you like to try driving?" she asked.

Lydia couldn't believe it! Sporting Ada's driving goggles she jumped in the driving seat, and after a few basic instructions and Henry turning the starting handle, she crunched a gear or two and lurched forward down the lane. Fortunately they encountered very little traffic of any kind, except for a startled cyclist, as she veered across the lane from one side to the other. Eventually, she drove all the way to Ombersley where they alighted to walk around the quaint little village.

Back in the car, Ada appraised Lydia for a brief moment. "I don`t know if you are aware of the fact, but you are quite beautiful, and beauty can be a curse. You are going to attract all sorts of attention, and I hope you are going to be able to deal with it. Jack for instance."

Lydia gripped the steering wheel tightly. "Jack and I are in love. But I suppose like his parents you disapprove."

"Personally, I can see you are meant for each other. But you will need to tread very carefully. Jack has confided in me that you have agreed to wait until he has finished university – or come up with some other plan, goodness knows what. I know you will find it difficult, but time apart will not be a bad thing…"

"Not a bad thing!" Lydia blurted out "You have no idea! It`s a very bad thing, a terrible thing! Social convention, position, snobbery that`s all it is! That`s the curse! Oh, I love him so much, Ada, you`ve no idea!"

Ada reached over and took the girl in her arms and Lydia cried as if her heart would break. It seemed a hopeless situation, but all the same in the short time she had known her, Ada was full of admiration for Lydia.

Eventually she said "Come on. You can keep up the act for a couple more hours. You have to."

*

Henry walked Jack down the lane a little prior to their departure.

"I have become very fond of you, Jack, we all have. Furthermore, it has not escaped my notice that … ahem … an attraction has developed between you and Lydia."

"Sir, I…" Jack began to protest.

"No, let me finish. I welcome your friendship with Alfred, and long may it continue. However, it pains me to request that you do not visit us again whilst you still harbour these…these obvious feelings for my daughter. Of course, if you were to become attached elsewhere, or Lydia was to find a … ahem, to become engaged herself, then that would be different."

Henry took a deep breath, and Jack, blushing to the roots of his hair, interjected quickly "It is true, Sir. There is a very strong mutual attraction between

112

Lydia and myself. When the time is right I intend to speak to my father. Perhaps then you will welcome me back to School House." If only Henry knew, he thought guiltily. But then, he fully intended to plead with his father again.

Henry considered this for a moment. "I hope you have not given Lydia cause for hopes in that direction, for I think it unlikely that anything will come of it."

He held out his hand. "Goodbye Jack, and good luck."

Minutes later, Jack gave Alfred a goodbye hug, and shook Eliza`s hand, then Lydia`s. He felt her tremble, and as he drew away he could see she that she had her eyes closed, as if she couldn`t bear to see him go. He himself had the devil`s own job to tear himself away. He thought of Shakespeare`s quote, "Parting is such sweet sorrow." There was nothing sweet about it at all.

It was very late when Ada and Jack arrived back in Leamington. Jack`s mother had retired, much to his relief, and they were in the sitting room having a nightcap, when the maid summoned Ada to the telephone. Jack heard her muffled voice in the hall, and looked up to see her return with a shocked look upon her face.

"Who was it?" asked Jack.

"It was your father. Tomorrow Great Britain will declare war on Germany."

Fourteen

"Oh, no! Not dear little Georgie. I can't bear it! And the baby too?" Lydia wept on her mother's shoulder. Little Georgie Amphlett and his baby sister had died of measles on the day that war was declared. This terrible tragedy overshadowed what seemed to everyone in Claines a far-off irrelevance.

"God help that poor mother." Eliza herself was near to tears.

The tragedy seemed doubly poignant and distressing for Lydia, for not only had she been very fond of the Georgie as her pupil, she would always remember Jack carrying him on his shoulders down the lane on that first Sunday after church.

At the funeral, Lydia watched Winnie the children's mother, stagger behind the sad little wooden coffins.

The following day there was a garden party at The Grange to which she and Alfred had been invited, but Lydia couldn't face it. Alfred attended, as he knew his friends Will and Lottie Shawcroft would be there. There had been a lot of talk there about the war, he told the family later, after supper.

"Apparently Charles Morris, who is in the Territorials, has reported to his regiment, and somebody said that Farmer Bryce from Tapenhall, who used to be in the Regulars, reported for service, but was turned down as he is too old."

Henry grunted in reply, and Eliza muttered something about men always being so keen to fight.

"Several of the young men are raring to go – you know – thinking about volunteering."

"I sincerely hope you have no such notions. You have an education to complete, and besides, it won't last long." Henry picked up his Berrow's Journal. "It is quoted here and I would agree;

'We are at war because Germany has chosen to test the powers and preparations she has been building to take her place in the sun.'"

He paused, then added, "Looks like the Three Choirs Festival may be postponed."

Alfred persisted. "Edwin said that he is seriously thinking about enlisting. He said several of the workers on the estate were thinking of volunteering, so it was up to people like him to lead by example."

"He's a fool. Let there be no more talk of enlisting. Great Britain has an army of professionals who will do their job. Together with the other allies we should send the Kaiser back home out of Belgium with his tail between his legs."

"I would get a commission father, like Edwin and Jack. We all have certificates granted by the Officer Training Corps of our public schools. What if the Kaiser doesn't retreat? I would have to do my duty."

Henry glared at him and grunted. "Hmmph. Just give it time, my boy, if it's not over by Christmas, then so be it."

Alfred turned to Lydia. "Edwin Bengeworth's face was like thunder when I had to give your apologies, Lyddy."

"That's another totally unsuitable young man who seems too interested in you, young lady. Just as well you didn't go," said Henry.

"And who might the other one be?" Lydia exclaimed.

Henry bristled. "You know very well of whom I speak! You should know that I have requested he has

115

nothing to do with you from now on." Henry rose from the table, as Lydia sat ashen-faced.

"But father …" began Alfred.

"He is your friend Alfred, and long may he remain so – away from this house. And that is an end to the matter." Henry left the table, and then they heard the door of the parlour slam shut. The three left at the table sat in silence for a few moments, until Eliza stood to clear the remaining cups from the table. She was concerned over Lydia; the children's deaths had left her in low spirits, and she knew that Henry's ultimatum had been a further shock. She would have to get Alfred to arrange an outing with Will and Lottie. Will Shawcroft would be eminently suitable for Lydia. She would get over Jack Albright in time.

Alfred persuaded Lydia to take a little walk in the garden.

"Cheer up, Lyddy. It's not the end of the world. I had a letter from Jack yesterday. He told me that Father had spoken to him …"

"So Jack has decided to forget me?"

"Oh no. On the contrary, he sounds bereft. He sent something in case a letter would incur father's wrath."

Lydia's eyes filled with tears.

"…well, anyway… I put it under your pillow."

Lydia blinked away her tears and sighed.

"I have to tell you this," Alfred continued. "It's not like father seems to think it is – you know, over there. Jack has sworn on the Bible to his father that he will wait until Christmas before enlisting, but it's killing him. Especially as his cousin Ada has already

116

left with the First Aid Nursing Yeomanry – the FANYS."

Lydia now gave him her full attention. "Ada?"

"Yes, well, I don`t know any more than that, just that she`s now in Belgium. She`s taken her Daimler to serve as an ambulance."

"When you write back to Jack tell him I`d love to hear from Ada. Wish I could go! What a brave person she is."

"Of course, Lyddy. And I`ll send Jack your love, shall I?"

"He has my love. Forever."

Lydia went to bed soon afterwards. She had her own bed back now, and she had not changed the pillow case that Jack had used; she now had a whole pillow to hug that still faintly held his scent. She felt underneath, and there it was, a folded piece of paper held together with sealing wax, for her eyes only.

"Stolen from Byron - To My Lady Lydia
There be none of Beauty's daughters
With a magic like thee;
And like music on the waters
Is thy sweet voice to me. – Always and Forever, J

Lydia clutched it to her heart. She stared into the darkness as her silent tears soaked the pillow. The funeral had depressed her; talk of war had depressed her. She desperately hoped that her father was right, that it would all be over soon. She couldn't bear to think of Alfred and Jack enlisting. Oh, no. That couldn't happen.

Two local companies of the 8th Battalion of the Worcestershire Regiment had paraded earlier in the week after war had been declared, headed by a Battalion Band. They marched from the Cross, up the High Street, through Sidbury to Crowle for a route march. They were part of the professional army that Henry referred to, but his prediction that the Kaiser would be sent packing proved unfounded.

Germany quickly and ruthlessly crushed Belgian resistance and marched into Brussels. The French offensive collapsed and the advancing German army left a trail of devastation and reported atrocities. The British expeditionary force fought a brave defensive battle south of Mons, but by the end of August, the Allied armies were floundering back on both and Eastern and Western fronts. Offensives and counter offensives were reported on both sides. By September the bright hopes of August lay trampled in the rain and mud.

A despondent Alfred returned to Oxford. He wrote home to Lydia that Jack was there too, and reported that the atmosphere at the University was highly charged - few were in the mood for study. Some of the dons who had been in the army had been recalled to their regiments, and young men from town and gown were volunteering in droves, responding to Lord Kitchener's call. He confided in Lydia that both he and Jack felt very frustrated, neither of them wanted to wait until Christmas.

By now, school had resumed and two of the older boys did not return. They had taken jobs at the Grange in the place of Tom Amphlett and Jim Stepford who had responded to the recruitment drive.

A desperate Lydia wrote back to Alfred, urging that he and Jack wait as promised.

Every day there was discussion after supper at School House about the war. Eliza had heard through Polly and others she met at the shops, about the increasing number of local young men volunteering. Henry would sigh as he read the increasing casualty lists reported in the Berrow's Journal, then retire sadly to the Parlour.

At the First Aid group, Lydia heard much talk about hospitals at the front; how more and more military nurses were being trained, and shipped over to France.

"I've been begging father to let me enlist in the Queen Alexandra's Imperial Military Nursing Service. They desperately need nurses," her friend Lizzie told her.

"If only I had your training Lizzie. What use is a teaching certificate at a time like this?"

Local hospitals all over the country were prepared in readiness for extra patients, and at the end of October Belgian troops were being treated at the Royal Infirmary. Local dignitaries began offering their houses and mansions for military hospitals if needed. Appeals went out for Voluntary Aid workers and many detachments began to be trained. Among the volunteers was Freddie.

"They wouldn't take me in the army," Freddie told Lydia sadly. "It's me foot of course. But I want to be of some use, so the Voluntary Aid Detachment's better than nothing. Mind you, the old man went mad."

"Why?" asked Lydia. He was giving her a lift back from her First Aid Group.

"Says I'm bloody stupid to volunteer for anything. 'Specially as I'm needed at home. Well now the harvest's over, and land work is drying up, he knows that's a load of nonsense. Can't see how much longer old Bessie's gonna last anyway. Poor old girl's really on 'er last legs. Gee up old Girl!"

Lydia knew it distressed Freddie to be taking Bessie out at all now, but Fred senior only caused the most almighty rows if he refused.

'ow's Master Alfred getting on - 'im and 'is friend Master Jack?"

"Oh, they're fine. Both of them are dying to join up, but they've both promised their parents to wait until after Christmas. But you have inspired me, Freddie. I shall offer my services at the Infirmary at the weekends!"

*

Two days later, Lydia received a letter postmarked from Flanders. She opened it carefully, trying to control her excitement, with Eliza and Henry peering over her shoulder. It was from Ada. She tactfully avoided mention of Jack. Lydia read aloud;

Alfred requested that I write to you, and I am delighted to do so, as it affords a welcome respite from the mayhem around us.

You must know that the government turned us down when we volunteered our services, so we have been working behind the Belgian lines. No-one – even those of us with experience in the hospitals – has been prepared for what we have found here. But believe me, we have learnt jolly quickly! We have helped set up soup kitchen and canteens, and some of the girls with nursing experience are working in the field hospitals. I knew my jaunts round the old country in my Daimler would come in useful! I brought the old Yellow Peril over here, and she did duty as an ambulance for a while until she was requisitioned by a French Officer. I`ve been driving Belgian ambulances since – dreadful old contraptions. At first they wouldn`t let us do much, but now we transport the wounded from the battlefields to the hospital. It gets frightfully hairy at times, the shells bursting around us, but some-one has to do it! Young ladies are turning up every week – a few have returned just as quickly too, as they can`t stand the rain, the mud and the blood. The reality of war is far too much for some of them. But, most do stay, and what brave girls they are!

Well, Lydia dear, I hope to come home for Christmas. No-one can stand this pace forever. The noise of the artillery alone is enough to drive you mad. God knows how the poor soldiers stand it. Those who survive. Their wounds are terrible, and they seem to be fighting relentlessly with very little success on either side. They are digging trenches now, on both sides. Don`t let anyone fool you, this war is going to be a long one. I do hope you are still attending your First Aid classes. Your skills will be needed in the months to come, for I`m sure you will want to help at your local hospital. They will be shipping men home soon.

Please write to me about Claines. Tell me about the walks to the river and about the children in school.

With much love to you and your dear parents…

Lydia stopped reading and looked at her astonished parents.

"What an incredibly brave woman, I can`t believe it!" said Eliza.

"If the Government didn't want the FANYS, then there must have been a good reason for it! It's bad enough the men putting their lives on the line, without silly society women doing so!" Henry shook his head. "All the same, such a brave woman. I don't know what to think. Women driving ambulances!" Deep in thought he made his way to school, Lydia trailing after him.

Later, in her room, Lydia wrote back to Ada, trying to make her trivial life sound interesting.

Then she wrote a short missive to Jack saying how much she missed him and still loved him; always and forever.

*

At the Ypres salient, on October 31st the Germans broke through the British Front at Gheluvelt. The situation was saved by the extraordinary bravery of the 2nd Royal Worcestershire Regiment who routed the enemy, and prevented them reaching the Channel Ports. The first Battle of Ypres continued until the middle of November and died away in stalemate. It also marked the end of the old British regular army for 58,000 officers and men had fallen. There was stalemate, and the trenches extended unremittingly from the North Sea to Switzerland.

Fifteen

"Oh, that`s a comfort, Molly" said Lydia, hugging a mug of weak, hot tea in Molly Ganderton`s cottage, on a cold, windy Saturday morning in November. She had trudged there to collect their weekly basket of eggs.

"`Course you`ve heard that the Amphlett children are now in the workhouse. Nothin` for it – poor old Jack gave his neck after Winnie died."

"Poor Sarah, and those little ones."

"Well we all did what we could, including you and yer mam, Miss. I feel sorry for young John `earing the news out in France. Give me regards to her ma. Your Alfred joined up yet, Miss?"

"No, not yet. We hope to have him home for Christmas, and then I suppose he`ll go like all the others."

She passed by the Maycroft`s cottage where all was quiet. Freddie now worked full time as a paid orderly at the Royal Infirmary, and received the first regular wages he had ever had. But apparently that still didn`t satisfy his father. She waved to Taffy Jones, hard at work at his forge. His son Tudor still helped him, but she knew he was under pressure to join up, but not from his father, as Taffy was a firm believer in conscription. "He has a young wife and son. He`ll go when they call him," he had told Lydia. They had both known it would not be long.

She walked back up the lane, holding her cloak tightly around her. She heard a horse clip-clopping towards her, but thought little of it, as she was too busy shielding her face from the biting wind.

"Good Morning, Miss Lydia." The horse and rider drew level with her, and she looked up to see Edwin Bengeworth smiling down at her. He turned his mare slightly into her path, so that she had to stop. Edwin was fully dressed in officer's uniform, and Lydia could not help but be impressed by the sight of him.

"So you've enlisted. Congratulations," Lydia said pleasantly.

"Yes, Indeed. Off to the south coast tomorrow for training. Itching to get over there and do my bit. Hope it won't be too long. Is Alfred still at Oxford?"

"Yes he is, but no doubt he will be going soon as well. He is very keen to do so."

"Well, who knows? Might be in the same regiment eh?"

"Perhaps. Well Edwin, I wish you luck." Lydia adjusted her hood, and turned to go.

Edwin bent down towards her, as he shifted the horse gently, blocking her way. There was the creak of leather, and the jingle of reigns. The mare snorted and tossed her head. Lydia stared at the straining muscles beneath its shining, chestnut coat. She reluctantly raised her eyes to meet Edwin's.

He steadied his mount and spoke to her gently.
"I'm really sorry we've never got to know each other better. You've turned down all my invitations."

"I have been busy - my job – and I volunteer at the Infirmary too."

"I would expect nothing less of you, my dear. You and all the other gallant ladies can be relied upon in our hour of need. You can be a great comfort..." He reached down and grabbed her hand,

and she gave a little cry that caused the horse to shift again, but Edwin held onto her hand.

"I`m sorry, I didn`t mean to frighten you. I mean you no harm, Lydia. I leave tomorrow. Will you meet me tonight?"

"What?" She tried in vain to wrench her hand free.

"Come to the back of the house tonight, I`ll meet you there, I`ll smuggle you in - don`t worry, I`ll look after you. Please. You must know I want you. Come to me, give me something to remember, something to look forward to when I get back."

Lydia was appalled and tried desperately to pull her hand away. The intense look on Edwin`s face frightened her, and so did the horse, who seemed to sense the atmosphere as she snorted and whinnied. Eventually he had to let go, as he fought to control his horse. An egg rolled off the top of the basket onto the floor.

He moved his mount aside to let her pass. "Perhaps you would feel more at home in the folly?" Seeing her shocked expression he laughed.

She clasped her hood tightly around her neck, and for a moment thought her trembling legs wouldn`t carry her forward. But somehow they did.

"Goodbye Miss Lydia! I shall have to make do with the memory of your lovely face to keep me warm at night."

Lydia turned when she knew she was a fair distance away. Edwin, proud and tall on his mare, saluted her with his swagger stick.

A few days before Christmas Alfred hauled his student's trunk into the small hallway of School House. There was no doubt that he would not be returning to Oxford.

"I shall be enlisting with the Worcesters after Boxing Day father," he announced, his head held high. Lydia and Eliza exchanged nervous glances, but Henry merely said, "so be it," and retired to the parlour.

Later the same day another letter arrived from Ada. They all sat round the kitchen table after supper and listened as Henry read aloud.

'As you can see by the address I have been back in England for a week now, and suffering from a bout of bronchitis.

My superiors thought I needed a rest and for once I decided to take their advice. Jack tells me he and Alfred plan to enlist. It is of course inevitable that our brave young men will want to fight for King and Country. I just pray with all my heart that God keeps them safe.

I shall be returning to Belgium myself as soon as I feel re-invigorated. A spot of fundraising in London should do the trick! I have a townhouse here and shall soon be in the thick of it.

Once again, do thank your parents for their hospitality back in the summer. My word, it does seem a long time ago! Do keep writing Lydia, your letters cheer me so.

"Extraordinary woman!" murmured Henry as he folded the letter. Must say that I still think Flanders is no place for a woman, but it seems that many like her are making a difference. Extraordinary."

Yes, extraordinary, mused Lydia. Women did go to war, and not only privileged, exceptional women like Ada. Her friend Lizzie had gone the week before with her nursing colleagues, and she knew from working at the Infirmary that many ordinary people had gone with the Voluntary Aid Detachments. Oh, why had she become a teacher and not a nurse? But perhaps… an idea began to form in her mind.

Alfred managed a moment alone with Lydia just before bedtime. He told her that Jack hoped to enlist in Worcester, and that he would move heaven and earth to try to see her. This was the news Lydia had been waiting for – he hadn't forgotten her.

"Of course not, sis. I must admit I had my doubts about Jack's sincerity at one time, but I do believe he loves you. I've slipped a missive under your pillow – and something else. 'Night Liddy."

Lydia closed her bedroom door and tore away her pillow. The envelope was thicker than usual, for inside there were three photographs, all obviously taken on their visit to the lakes. Two were of Alfred and Jack, carefree and windblown, the hills as a backdrop. There was also one of Jack alone. Jack, her beloved, handsome Jack. The sight of his image overwhelmed her – she sobbed into her pillow until she felt her heart would break. It was much later that she read Jack's words taken from Wordsworth.

Dearest Lydia,
I dream of you, I long for you. Until we meet
Again you shall be
'the anchor of my purest thoughts, the nurse,
The guide, the guardian of my heart and soul,
Of all my moral being.' - Always and Forever, J

The family made the most of Christmas; they had a goose for lunch and a plum pudding to follow. They lit the candles on their tiny tree in the parlour and gathered to exchange their small gifts. Henry took great pride in presenting Alfred with a fine Hunter watch.

"My father gave it to me on my twenty first birthday. This is a little early I know, but well, an officer should have a fine timepiece."

Alfred handed Lydia a small padded box, and her parents gasped when she opened it to reveal a large oval gold locket on a chain.

"But Alfred, it…it`s so lovely, so expensive…"

Alfred blushed. "All that glisters is not gold, silly girl. Good imitation though, don`t you think?"

A tiny shudder of relief passed over them all.

Henry poured the ladies sherry and a generous glass of port for himself and Alfred. He raised his glass.

"To absent friends."

As they repeated the toast, Lydia, of course, thought of Jack.

On her way to bed, she picked up Ada`s letter and in her room copied down her London address.

*

On Boxing Day Lydia accompanied Alfred into Worcester. He told his parents that he wanted to treat his sister to lunch at The Star, the best hotel in Worcester. Henry thought it amazingly extravagant and unnecessary, but Eliza persuaded him that it was a loving gesture.

So Lydia donned a smart new fashionable navy-blue woollen suit with a white cotton lawn blouse for the outing to lunch. She tied a little fur tippet round her neck, and her hands trembled slightly as she adjusted her matching wide-brimmed fur hat in the mirror. The clothes were the most expensive she could afford on her small salary, and had purchased them with Jack in mind. And he was very much on her mind today, for he would be meeting them.

Alfred bristled with pride, as he escorted his sister into the dining room, and there, pushing his chair back to stand and welcome them to their table was Jack. Lydia's legs felt like jelly, but somehow she kept her composure. Jack took her hand, and greeted her with a brotherly kiss, then hugged Alfred. Lydia sat down almost in a trance. Surely they could all hear her heart beating?

"Well, here we are then! Isn`t this splendid? And you, Lydia, you look wonderful…" Jack, as ever, was not lost for words.

For what seemed like an eternity the two lovers seemed lost in their own world as Alfred ordered food and wine. Eventually Jack and Lydia relaxed and included Alfred in their conversation, but Alfred seemed resigned to play the part of chaperone. When Lydia looked back on this meeting, she was unable to remember any of the conversation or anything she ate. She was only aware of the thudding of her heart and Jack. She took in every detail of him. He was still clean shaven, but his hair was much shorter. As he talked she watched every detail of his face, how his brown eyes crinkled at the sides when he smiled, the line of his jaw that she longed to trace with her finger. And that smile! Those generous lips that she longed to kiss. And he looked at her in exactly the same way when their eyes met. As she smiled, nibbled her food or made some inane comment, all she could think was; "let him still love me. Please God let him still think me beautiful."

They left Alfred in the bar of the hotel and went for a walk along the River Severn, in the shadow of the Cathedral. The leaden sky matched the grey waters. Jack told her how much he missed her, and that he had found it almost impossible to make small talk at lunch. All he could think about was her, and the overwhelming urge that he had felt to stroke her face and kiss her lips.

They sat on a riverside bench, and at last he took her in his arms and kissed her.

"My darling, I love you so much, I want you so much. I have a room at the hotel. Will you come back there with me?"

Lydia felt the now familiar surge of desire almost overwhelm her. "Oh Jack, if only I could..."

"There is no other way we can be together."

"I know, but... No, how can I? How can you ask it of me?"

He held her tight. "I'm sorry Lyddy. Oh, it's so wrong of me, but I want you so much. After I enlist, God knows when I'll see you again."

They embraced for a long time, until they heard Alfred cough nearby. "Come on you two. Time to get back."

Alfred walked ahead and the lovers walked back to the hotel arm in arm. Lydia felt the world could judge her; she couldn't pretend any more today.

"I see you are wearing my locket," said Jack. "It was the only way I could think of giving you a present that you could wear openly. Alfred bought the chain." They shared a final embrace.

Later, in her room, Lydia took out of her box the photograph of Jack and Alfred, and cut out their faces, placing the photographs in her locket. Somehow she had known that the locket was as genuine as their love for each other.

They had said their good byes and knew that they would not meet again before he went to war. War – how had it all come to this? Please God keep them safe. She finally fell asleep at last clutching the locket and lost herself in dreams of Jack.

Sixteen

Lydia wrote in her journal:

`I have to go to France, and the only way is to somehow qualify as a nurse, or become a full-time member of the V.A.D. My other plan is to write to Ada. Perhaps I could join the FANYS, or she could know some other way of my helping in France or Flanders. The newspapers tell of how sorely pressed the London hospitals are with injured troops transferred from the front. Lizzie has already gone, and says how desperate they are for volunteers, but father will not even discuss the subject. Even so I intend to keep trying.`

Alfred wrote from `somewhere on the South Coast`, but as yet no mention was made of leaving for overseas.

Lydia tried again, but Henry was resolute.

"Just because you`ve got a couple of First Aid Certificates doesn`t mean that you`ll be of any earthly use with soldiers suffering from shrapnel wounds and with limbs shot off! Besides, you are needed at school!"

The next day walking home with Freddie after a voluntary Saturday shift at the infirmary, Polly met them in the Lane.

"Lydia`s going to France, Polly. She`s going out with the V.A.D.s" said Freddie.

"Oh is she? And what d`ye think your father will think of that Miss Lydia?"

Lydia ignored Polly`s hostile tone. "He doesn`t know yet – and you`re not to breathe a word! I know Polly, why don`t we go together?"

"To France? Oh, no Miss, you must be mad. And me mam would kill me, `specially now our Albie and

Hal have enlisted. Besides I couldn't stand it, they only get the filthy jobs to do – I don`t know how you can do it."

"I seem to have a strong stomach – but when you`re helping the patients, knowing that they need you – well somehow it`s all worthwhile."

Freddie looked at Lydia dreamily. "Yeah, I do know what you mean."

"You must have that in mind when you`m moppin` up the blood and guts from the operatin` theatre, then Freddie?" said Polly.

"Well somebody has to do it," he shrugged.

"Exactly!" said Lydia. "And if I have to do nothing but mop up blood in some field hospital, and bandage broken limbs, I will. After all, it may be Alfred`s broken limbs."

"Or Master Jack`s," said Polly quietly.

"Well I think you`m very brave Lydia. To think of goin` out there when you could just carry on as normal here."

Polly sighed as she watched Lydia smile condescendingly at Freddie. He still worshipped the ground Lydia walked on. She wished she would go tomorrow. Typical of her. Who`d want to risk their lives working in a field hospital? She just couldn't help being excitable, always wanting to be the centre of attention. Probably more to it, knowin` her. Probably thinks she can chase after Master Jack or something. And Freddie as usual thought she was some kind of `eroine. So she was brave eh? What did that make her, `carrying on as normal here?`A coward? She`d have it out with Freddie later on.

Just then a loud wailing halted all further discussion. They ran past the blacksmith's on the corner and saw Taffy and Freda Jones just inside Bessie's stable next to Freddie's cottage. The wailing was coming from Freda.

Freddie called out "What's up?" as he limped up to them, and Polly and Lydia stood back. Two of the Ganderton children stood at the bottom of the garden with their mother.

Old Bessie was lying in the straw, her flanks streaked with blood. At her side was Fred senior, his body twisted and his head thrown back, a pool of blood beginning to congeal around his head. Freddie's mother was sitting on a little stool next to him, staring at him and mumbling. She had a large wooden mallet in her hand. Lydia shouted for someone to fetch Dr.Moreton.

Freddie gently took the mallet from his mother, and laid it on the floor.

"What happened mam?" Freddie said.

"I told the bugger I'd swing for 'im. Well, I swung for 'im alright."

"Mam, what have you done?"

Aggie stared at the horse. "Beat that poor old girl once too often. She couldn't get up, I told 'im. Bin a good old girl she 'as. You knows that Fred. It was 'er and you what kept us alive, with enough left over for 'im to get drunk every night."

Poor Freddie looked up in horror at Polly and Lydia. Lydia and Taffy exchanged glances. Some instinct made Lydia kick the mallet under the straw.

"Must 'ave been a shock to find him like this missus." Taffy said gently. "Old Bessie must 'ave caught him off guard. `Spose after all these years, she`d just about `ad enough. Caught `im in her death throes, eh? `Ere Freddie, give us a hand. Can`t leave `im `ere like that."

He motioned for Freddie to help, and together they carried Fred into the house. He nodded to Lydia, as they walked past. Polly and Freda lifted Aggie gently from the milking stool, and they followed. Molly Ganderton drifted off mumbling "poor old Bessie wouldn`t `urt a fly," just as Dr. Moreton came bustling up the path.

Lydia gave the doctor a quick explanation of what she thought had happened, then she went back into the stable. She covered up the blood stains with straw, then pushed the mallet into a pile of garden rubbish behind the stable. She joined the others in the parlour, where Dr. Moreton was examining the back of Fred`s head as he lay on the old horsehair sofa.

"Nothing I can do for him now, I`m afraid." He glanced round at Aggie who was sitting by the fireplace, staring into space. "Old Bessie kicked him, you say?"

"I think she`s in shock now Doctor. But she did tell us that, before you got here." Lydia looked away from Polly, who stared at her, aghast.

"Old Bessie must `ave dropped dead straight after. Can`t get a word out of me mam since." Freddie said.

"You`re right, she`s in shock. Give her time." He closed his black bag, and Polly gave him his hat. "I`ll contact Timmins," he said referring to the undertaker. "Good day. I`m very sorry for your loss."

135

Lydia escorted him out, her legs feeling like jelly. She held her breath as he peered over the stable door. It began to really dawn on her the seriousness of what she had done. The doctor shook his head. "Extraordinary. Can`t believe the old girl had that much strength in her."

Back in the cottage Lydia offered to fetch old Mrs.Thompson, who traditionally did the `laying out` of the dead in the parish.

"No," Polly was quick to reply. "Me and Fred can do it."

"I`ll help" said Lydia.

"No. It`s alright Miss. This is family business. Just you get off `ome now. I think you`ve done enough."

There was no mistaking the note of hostility in Polly`s voice. Freddie walked up to Lydia and took her hand.

"Thanks, Miss Lydia. Thanks for your help." Then he looked at Taffy and Freda, who were still standing silently behind the sofa. "Thanks Taffy" he said. Taffy just nodded. They all stood in silence for a moment. They all knew they shared a terrible secret.

When the others had left, Polly went to the scullery and filled a kettle for boiling, cursing Lydia Winters under her breath. What the devil did she cover it all up for? Trust `er and `er do goodin` ways.

*

After the bleak little funeral, which Aggie refused to attend, Polly avoided Lydia at School House as much as she could. The secret of that evening had become an unspoken barrier between the two girls, which

Lydia found hard to understand. Then one day, out of the blue, Polly announced to Eliza and Lydia that she and Freddie were to be married the following month. After they had both congratulated her, Lydia followed her out to the washing line.

"I'm so pleased for you Polly."

"You sounds surprised Miss. Well, I suppose you would be, to think that Freddie could be 'arbouring feelings of affection for anybody else, besides yourself that is."

Lydia stared at her with horror. "Freddie? Freddie and me?"

"You must 'ave known that he worships the flippin' ground you walk on."

"Does he? No, no … Oh Polly, we've always been friends, since we were little …"

"And then you grew up and became the village teacher. I work for you and yer mam, and Freddie runs errands for you all. Didn't stop 'im adorin' you though, - I used to see the little looks he gave you, and you 'im."

Lydia was appalled. "Oh, Polly. I love Freddie, we all do, as a dear friend. I hope I never led him on, but I never dreamt that he had hopes…you know…of anything more."

"Course he didn't. But what's the old sayin'? 'A cat can look at a Queen'? summat like that. 'Ent that a bit like you and Master Jack? But I suppose you 'ent given up 'opes of 'im – well good luck to ya. But me and Freddie, I suppose the difference is, Miss, we knows our place. We likes each other well enough. The only thing stoppin' us was his parents. But now…well there's nothing stoppin' us now."

She chewed her lip for a second. "Thing is though, we're gonna be lumbered with mad Aggie, whereas if you 'adn't interfered, we'd have bin shot of the both of 'em."

"Oh Polly! It just seemed the best thing to do. Taffy took over really…."

"Yeah, but as usual, you just 'ad to join in. If you 'adn't I'd have stopped 'im. I'd 'ave 'ad 'er carted off to clink, or the loony bin. She deserved it."

Lydia had been suffering pangs of guilt and sleepless nights since the whole episode, but she had no idea that Polly felt like this. Oh, why had she interfered?

"I only acted on instinct – to protect Freddie mainly. Think of the shame and humiliation he would feel if people knew the truth."

Polly started pegging out the washing. "He'd have got over it. It was his chance for a new start. Now we'll 'ave 'er round our necks for God knows 'ow long."

"I can't turn the clock back Polly. You have to believe that I wanted to protect Freddie and his mother. I don't think we should talk of this again."

She walked away with her head held high, but felt as if her heart was breaking. She was losing everyone she loved. She had to get away. That night she wrote to Ada in London, telling her of her frustrations and desire to help with the war effort. Could she join the FANYS and go back to Belgium with Ada?

*

The wedding was a short, simple affair two weeks before Easter. Polly looked pretty in her best muslin dress, and somehow Freddie looked so tall and proud as he walked with his bride up the aisle; it seemed to Lydia that he hardly limped at all.

*

Alfred's battalion was still training in southern England, and Lydia furtively collected a letter from Jack from the Post Office, giving her similar news and confirming his love for her. She also received a reply from Ada telling her emphatically that Flanders really was no place for Lydia, which left her bitterly disappointed.

Henry regularly read aloud to them from his newspaper about the scandal of the shell shortages at the front. Then, at the end of April, yellow clouds of chlorine gas was released by Germany towards the Allied Troops at the second bloody battle of Ypres. And still the stalemate continued, with offensive and counter offensive and massive loss of life. The recruiting for Lord Kitchener's Army continued in earnest.

Lydia celebrated her nineteenth birthday quietly in May, and to her delight there was a card for her at the post office. Jack had sent a card with an embroidered forget-me-not on the front, with the words;-

'The flowers say it all. Always and forever, Jack.'

Life plodded on in Claines. The good ladies of the parish, including Eliza, were regularly involved in holding teas and sales of work. They made small garments for children, as the number of war widows increased. Lydia took part in several choral concerts to raise funds. Her job and voluntary activities ensured that every waking hour was filled with some industry; she felt she would go mad if she had too much time to think.

*

In the middle of June, Alfred returned home for a few days' embarkation leave. He would be leaving for The Dardanelles in Turkey. He took Lydia to the Theatre Royal with Will and Lottie. The two boys looked grand in their sub-lieutenant's uniforms, and the girls were proud to be with them. Will was leaving for France and was a fine fellow, but Lydia couldn't help wishing that Jack was sitting in his place.

Under the pillow that night she found a note that Alfred had left from Jack - a pressed buttercup with the simple words;

My Lady;
'Another flower from another crannied wall'
Until we meet again,
Always and forever, Jack.'

Dear God, keep him safe she prayed.

Seventeen

By July Lydia knew that Jack and Alfred were heading for Gallipoli, and Lizzie was nursing in northern France, from where she wrote that "nothing could have prepared me for the terrible conditions here."

"Surely this should convince you of the foolishness of volunteering," her father said. "Like the rest of us, your place is here, whether you like it or not!"

"My place? Everyone is so keen to keep me in place! Well, it doesn`t feel like I`m in place at all! My destiny is elsewhere, I need to go Father, I want to nurse. Please let me go!"

"Destiny! Balderdash! You read too much young lady! I think you`d better stick to rolling bandages with the ladies of the parish and stop going to the infirmary. You`ll go abroad over my dead body! Now, leave this room, and let it be an end to the matter. Am I not master in my own house?"

Henry started coughing, and Eliza had to settle him down with a glass of water, waving Lydia away. Near to tears, she closed the kitchen door. Nevertheless her father`s opposition only seemed to spur her on. She was destined never to please him anyway. She quietly slipped into the parlour and removed an old tin box from his writing desk. It only took her a few seconds to find her birth certificate.

Tomorrow was Saturday – and tomorrow she would set out for London, and then out to France, or even the Dardanelles, for that`s where she wanted to be, near Alfred and Jack. Her parents would be devastated, but so be it. She was going for Jack and

Alfred, she was going for the boys out there, and she was going for herself.

She took out her box of letters and poems and re-read them for the umpteenth time. She placed them with the photograph of Jack into the back of her journal. She re- read the first page. That day with Alfred and Jack walking through the barley field - how he had compared her to the Lady of Shalott. Their eyes had met and she knew from that moment she was his. Just a year ago. She wondered if they would ever go punting down the Cherwell, or see the fritillaries in the Oxford meadow.

She also remembered those two fine boys shouting out verses of the Charge of the Light Brigade and shivered. Now they were truly brothers in arms.

It was barely light when she crept down the stairs, holding her breath, convinced that every creak of the staircase would stir her parents. She struggled down Cornmeadow Lane, hot already in her navy blue suit, clutching her valise in one hand which contained her precious box, and an old carpet bag of her mother's into which she had packed her spare underclothes, skirt and blouse. Thankfully, she passed no-one she knew. She stopped at the Green and slipped a note to Freddie asking him to pass on a letter to her parents.

At Foregate Street Station, as she boarded the early train going to London; she was excited and filled with trepidation at the same time. She gazed out at the green countryside and the cloud-filled sky, but didn't search for signs or omens. She was afraid of what she might see.

When she stepped off the train at Paddington, she was totally disorientated. The noise of the engines, the smoke and press of people almost overwhelmed her. She eventually made her way through the throng of people – including many men in various regimental uniforms.

Once outside the station she faltered. She only had some vague notion of finding a hospital where she could offer her services.

She struggled along the busy streets – there was so much traffic – still many horse-drawn vehicles, but more cars and even double-decker omnibuses. She came to an even busier road which she could see by a corner sign was the Bayswater Road, and there was a bus stop. She resolved to wait until she saw a bus with a name displayed that she recognised. Soon one did stop, its destination -Trafalgar Square. She felt her old optimism re-surface; she was in London, the capital city.

Sitting on top of the open omnibus she stared down in awe at the sweeping acres of Hyde Park, then the grandeur of Marble Arch. A woman took her fare. She had read that women were starting to take the place of men in many jobs, in factories, on the buses and on the land.

She became absorbed in watching the life of the city around her – the magnificent buildings and shops, so many fine ladies and gentlemen, so many top hats! And then … Nelson`s Column.

She scrambled down the bus steps and just stared in fascination at the grandeur before her that was Trafalgar Square. She was just about to cross the busy road to get there, when another sight along the road rooted her to the spot. It took a few seconds for her to realise what she was seeing – to realise that the blend of bodies in dirty khaki was a great mass of wounded men gathered all together. She stared and stared trying to take it in. She eventually realised that they were outside another railway station – Charing Cross.

"Shockin' sight innit lav?"

She turned, hardly understanding the strange accent. It was a newspaper seller. She nodded.

"Bringin' em in fwom over there. Wish I could get me 'ands on just one o' them 'uns. Trouble is, lost me old leg to the Boer," he tapped his wooden leg.

Lydia stared at the stump, then over to the mass of wounded, and had to suppress the urge to run. She took a deep breath and eventually plucked up courage and asked the man if he would look after her bags and jacket for a while. He nodded and tucked her belongings down behind his little newspaper box.

As she got to the crowded forecourt she could see a few nurses patiently moving among the wounded men, who were lying or squatting on the ground. Others with Red Cross armbands were taking round tea and water.

A soldier, sitting on the floor next to a wounded comrade on a stretcher looked up at her. His face and uniform were caked in mud, and his arm was in a sling, dried blood staining the filthy bandage. He was clutching his stomach, where she noticed another blood soaked dressing. The fetid smell was like nothing she had ever experienced. She felt the nausea rising in her throat.

144

"S`aright luv, we`re pretty `armless – and legless some of us! Ha!" She put her hand to her mouth.

"Oi!" She spun round to see an angry male V.A.D. orderly staring at her.

"What d`ya fink you`re doin`? Clear off, this ain`t a bloody side-show!" Then she was pushed aside as two stretcher bearers waded into the melee towards a doctor standing with his hand raised. She staggered back, looking once more at the soldier`s empty eyes. He looked away from her and spat.

Swallowing back the bile in her mouth and the urge to scream, she made her way back to the newspaper vendor.

"Now, just what did you fink you was gonna do, lav?"

"I-I thought I might help… I came to be a nurse." Her voice sounded pathetic against the hustle and noise. My God! If they were in this state here, whatever must it be like on the battlefields, in the trenches, in the field hospitals?

"If I was you, lav, I`d get back `ome where you belong. Leave all that to them as knows."

Yes, he was right. She knew nothing. "Thank you for looking after my things," she said, near to tears. She collected her case and jacket, and walked on in a daze. She had to bite back the tears of self-pity and the instinct to get straight back on a train to Worcester. No, she should revert to her original plan and find a hospital. Surely they would be glad of any help at all? She dropped her things on the floor and leant against a doorway.

"You awright duckie?" A large, rosy faced woman put her hand on Lydia`s shoulder and smiled.

Lydia was transfixed by her cheeks – surely not naturally red, and her rotting teeth.

"I - I wonder if you could direct me to the nearest hospital?"

"'Course I can duckie. 'Ere, let me 'elp you wiv ya bags." Lydia let her take the carpet bag, but instinctively grabbed her small valise. She was used to seeing poverty in Claines, but the stench from this woman made her hold her breath as she led her along the Strand. After a hundred yards or so, the woman turned and said "You wait 'ere duckie. My bruvver's a cabbie, 'e can take you the rest of the way." And before Lydia could protest, the woman disappeared down an alleyway. It was over half an hour later, when it dawned on Lydia that the woman had stolen her bag and would not be returning. She ventured down the alleyway – which led to another, then a warren of walkways and decrepit buildings – a public house where several disreputable looking men made lewd comments to her. Somehow, she managed to retrace her steps to the Strand, clutching her valise, so grateful that she still had its contents and her few shillings. How on earth would she survive in this frightening, hostile city? She was too proud to return home, but she knew more than ever that she needed help, and in her valise she had Ada's address.

She found a taxi rank and very soon she was standing on the pavement in Grosvenor Crescent, having spent one of her precious shillings on a cab. Grand Georgian houses, with their pillars, black railings and clean steps led to imposing front doors; and there were many trees in full summer bloom.

She regarded the polished black door of number five, walked tentatively up the steps, and knocked.

The door was opened by an elderly female servant whose cold eyes swiftly appraised Lydia.

"Tradespeople at the BACK door," she barked, and began to close the door.

"Oh, please, where is the back door? And…and is Miss Chellingworth at home?"

"Mrs. Harding! Who is it? I have told you time and again, some of my gals get hold of my address and I`d rather you didn`t turn them away."

The door opened wider once more and there stood Ada, resplendent in a severe purple costume and feathered hat, which she was in the process of pinning to her hair. Lydia had never been so pleased to see a familiar face in all her life.

"Lydia! What on earth are you doing here?"

"I…I`m so sorry Miss Chellingworth, I didn`t know where else to go. You see, I…I've left home. You know I want to nurse, and my father…well, you know my father - and Jack and Alfred are out there fighting and the other boys, and…and I've seen them Miss…Ada, I've seen them at the station, and oh, I must help. I can help can`t I?"

"Oh, my dear girl! Come inside before you collapse on me! Mrs. Harding, stop gaping and get the girl a cup of tea!"

"Shall I take her to the kitchen m`lady?" Mrs. Harding asked.

"Indeed you won't! Tea and sandwiches I think, as quick as you can - in the drawing room!"

Ada herself took Lydia`s coat and helped the exhausted girl through the hallway into the drawing room.

Lydia fought back her tears – she felt a combination of relief and exhaustion, but eventually she managed to recount the events of the past twenty-four hours, and repeat her determination to go across the channel and nurse at one of the hospitals there.

"I`m so sorry to turn up on your doorstep like this, and I know I can`t join the FANYs but there must be a way."

"You are so fortunate to find me still here! My departure has been delayed and I`m on my way to one of my fund raising events – a concert at the Albert Hall…" She turned to the clock on the ornate mantelpiece. "… and I must fly. These events are so necessary. Ah, Mrs. Harding!"

The housekeeper placed a tray piled high with sandwiches, cakes and pretty cups and teapot, on a side table, and stood very straight and disapproving at its side.

"Now make sure Miss Lydia eats plenty won't you? Then air the blue room. Miss Lydia is to be our guest. I must go – ring Charters for the car will you?"

"Yes m`lady. And shall I run a bath for our guest m`lady?"

Lydia cringed and withered beneath the housekeeper`s knowing glance.

"In due course." Ada pulled on her gloves. "Now eat up young lady, then have that bath and go to bed.

I shall be late returning home. We`ll talk about all this tomorrow."

Left alone in the sumptuous room, Lydia did indeed feel very grubby and out of place, sitting in an over-stuffed armchair covered in some luxurious shiny fabric that matched other items in the room. There were thick, patterned carpets, heavy curtains, golden framed portraits around the walls, and exquisite vases and ornaments placed on antique furniture. She thought of the parlour at School House, and her mother`s few treasured keepsakes. Mrs. Harding was right to see her as a lower class interloper. That`s exactly what she was. And then it hit her, like a blow to her solar plexus. This was Jack`s world too. How could she ever hope to fit in? What on earth was she doing here?

Eighteen

Ada expected Lydia to return home within a day or two, chastened by the effects of her disastrous first day in London. But she soon discovered that Lydia was made of stronger stuff. In spite of the fact that Lydia only possessed the clothes she stood up in, she begged Ada to direct her to a hospital where she could volunteer as a VAD. Ada detected a kindred spirit – she had been impressed by the girl when she had met her in Claines, but had never expected their paths to cross again. She doubted that she would survive nursing abroad, but perhaps she could help her find a local hospital - eventually.

"First things first," she told Lydia the following morning. "I shall write to your parents to let them know you are safe, then we need to get you some decent clothes. The hospital I have in mind will not be recruiting for a month, so meanwhile I shall put you to work in return for bed and board and clothes."

"But I only need a VAD uniform," said Lydia, tucking her scuffed boots under Ada`s beautifully upholstered chair.

"Just trust me, my dear. My embarkation for Belgium has been delayed, but there is plenty for me to be going on with here. My last Girl Friday left a month ago, and my affairs are in a bit of a state. Now, let`s go shopping for those clothes."

Ada took her to Selfridges, a sumptuous department store the likes of which Lydia had never encountered. Back in Worcester she had visited their modest department store to purchase mainly ribbons, stockings and material, for her mother hand made all her garments. That had been the height of Lydia`s previous shopping experience. But now as until Ada whisked her through section after section of luxury goods, she felt overwhelmed by the sparkle, glow, whisper and smells of affluence. When her worn boots sank into the thick carpet of the couture department, and her eyes met those of the sales assistant, she wanted to run – or curl up and die with embarrassment, for this superior young lady recognised her for what she was; a poor little school marm totally out of her depth. But Ada soon put Miss Smith in her place, and Lydia was whisked into a small room and soon emerged decked out in a smart pale blue linen suit. Ada nodded her approval, and they repeated the process with four day dresses, a modest crepe de chine evening dress and matching hats and gloves. Lydia was breathless, but more was to come.

"Now Miss Smith, please bring us a selection of undergarments for my ward to choose from."

Lydia blushed as delicate silk French knickers, chemises and corsets were gently laid before her. She had no idea such finery existed. She wondered what Miss Smith had thought of her flannel drawers and worn chemise.

"We`ll take three sets, one in each colour", Ada said airily, then whispered to Lydia "I never wear anything else but silk next to my skin. You`ll love it too."

Ada was so full of surprises, thought wide-eyed Lydia.

Still feeling she was in a dream, she floated down the stairs two hours later, wearing her new suit; her elegant, pale beige buttoned court shoes sinking into the rich carpet. Miss Smith gave her a condescending parting smile. At least Lydia felt she now matched her lavish surroundings, and she lifted her chin determined to act the part of Miss Chellingworth's `ward`.

"It`s how I think of you now my dear," explained later as they sat in the drawing room. "I do rather feel in the role of `in loco parentis`, and I really am loving every moment!"

"I don`t know how to thank you Ada. I had no intention of putting you to all this trouble, all this expense …" she indicated the parcels which had just been delivered, containing the new dresses, hats, gloves, stockings and the undergarments which she couldn`t wait to try on.

"Today was wonderful my dear. This war has taught me one very important lesson; to live in the moment. Fate has thrown us together and for now it is my greatest wish to see you enjoy some comfort and pleasure in being a young lady. Mind you, you will be a lady who will earn her keep, I assure you!"

"Oh, anything Ada! I`ll try my very best not to let you down."

Later, Ada paused in the doorway on her way to bed and glanced in to see Lydia smoothing down her new skirt, then lift it a little to twist her ankle and admire her new shoes. "Please God let her enjoy all this, and the new role I will find for her. Anything to stop this foolish desire to run off and nurse," she prayed.

As promised, Lydia was soon set to work sorting out Ada`s chaotic paperwork and book keeping. She rattled collection boxes at rallies and with several other young ladies made regular trips to Victoria Station where they handed out tea and Bovril to the walking wounded from `over there`. One of these young ladies, Hermione Templeton, a tiny, fiery ex-debutante with wild hair and a raucous laugh, became a firm friend of Lydia`s despite their different backgrounds. Hermione also wanted to volunteer as a VAD.

Ada persuaded Lydia to accompany her to the occasional social event, and as Lydia descended the staircase dressed for an evening choral concert in her crepe de chine evening dress, Ada realised how far she had come in a short time.

"You look quite ravishing young lady."

Lydia blushed and touched her hair, now dressed in curls high on her head. "But it`s all thanks to you Ada. The clothes and the attention of the hairdresser. How can I ever repay you?"

"You are repaying me, every day my dear. Your help has been invaluable. Personally I find all this attention to female frippery rather tiresome. I subject myself to similar administrations, but I fear a silk purse cannot be made out of a sow`s ear."

"Oh, Ada, you have such style and…"

"Mmm. Let`s just say I rather prefer my jodhpurs and tin hat! Now, please understand that it gives me enormous pleasure to see someone with such natural elegance and beauty enhanced by a bit of pampering and style." Besides, she thought to herself, it would never do for Lydia to be dressed in the simple clothes of a village girl as her companion. In a short time she had become extremely fond of her and she could easily be her niece. Yes, giving Lydia ambition and the wherewithal to conduct herself in more sophisticated circles would do her no harm at all.

"You know you will turn every male head in your vicinity my dear. Come."

Lydia paused. "But there is only one male on my mind, Ada, you must know that."

"Of course. Well he would be very proud of you my dear. Nothing more after that last letter two weeks ago?"

Lydia nodded sadly and recalled the only letter she had received, months after it had been written, when Jack's regiment had been sailing towards Greece.

He had quoted Byron;

> *The Isles of Greece, the Isles of Greece!*
> *Where burning Sappho loved and sang.*

He wrote of his memories of times spent together – his longing to see her again, and his astonishment to hear of her living in London with Ada, and her dream of becoming a nurse.

Lydia began to wonder if she would ever realise that dream, when, out of the blue one day she returned from tea duty and Ada met her in the hallway dressed in her FANY uniform.

"Sudden orders to leave – just off, so glad to see you before I go," she embraced Lydia as Charters bustled in to pick up her trunk.

"Don't worry, Mrs. Harding and Charters will look after you, and she knows that you are to treat this house as your own in my absence." Thankfully, over the weeks the housekeeper had begun to warm towards her.

"Now you're quite used to the routine. Not too much paperwork now, but keep up with the collections and Station visits. What you do is so important you know. Toodle pip!"

*

So Ada left, feeling confident that Lydia was well ensconced in the useful niche she had created for her. She had however, underestimated Lydia's determination who had grown very close to Hermione. A week later her friend called at the house bursting with exciting news.

"My cousin has got us places at a hospital Lydia! We can start as Voluntary Aid nurses next week!"

And so it was that within days Lydia and Hermione found themselves scurrying along the bare, disinfected corridors and wards of the Royal London hospital.

For the next six months they hardly drew breath. All VADs lived in, sleeping in large dormitories, and any romantic ideas Lydia had of nursing wounded soldiers (in spite of Ada doing her hardest to dispel any such romantic notions) were hardly realised at first, for most of the work consisted of scrubbing floors on her hands and knees, carrying and sterilising instruments, flourishing mops, buckets and blankets, and worst of all working in the sluice room where she had nearly fainted at the sight and smells of severed arms, legs and unidentifiable lumps of flesh in buckets, waiting to be disposed of. On top of that, she found that the VADs were very much looked down on by the regular nurses. Sometimes she thought perhaps her father had been right, and she frequently missed the comfort of life with Ada.

But whenever she wavered, the support and companionship of Hermione got her back on track.

Eventually Lydia was helping to change dressings and assist occasionally in the operating theatre. She and some of the other girls also gave some of their precious spare time helping some of the barely literate boys compose letters to their mothers, wives and sweethearts.

Ada had never received a reply from her parents, and neither had Lydia who wrote weekly. She had also told Polly about becoming a VAD at last, and eventually had a reply.

` Freddie and me and his mam are alright. I have started a job at the cartridge factory in Blackpole as the money is good. Sarah Amphlett has come to live with us from the workhouse and has started as housemaid at School House. Her brother John was killed in France. So far my brothers are alright. We hope that Master Alfred and Master Jack keep safe. Your mam says she will never forgive you and I can understand. I hope nothing happens to you But I don`t want to write no more.

Lydia sighed, but no longer felt hurt. She had new friends and important work to do. Polly belonged to the life she had left behind. Besides, there was no time for anything else but the unremitting slog and toil of hospital duties. She was determined to stay focussed; this is what she had wanted. Somehow and sometime in the near future she would be helping boys like Jack, and maybe, just maybe she secretly hoped, it could all take her to Jack himself, couldn't it?

Nineteen

On their days off the girls caught up on their sleep, and occasionally Hermione took Lydia home to tea, or they visited the art galleries and museums that Jack had talked to her about, but she never managed to find Waterhouse's Lady of Shalott. Oh, it all seemed such a long time ago!

She dropped in to see Mrs. Harding who nodded in disapproval at her uniform. "After all Miss Chellingworth did to turn you into a lady!"

Lydia did in truth often feel a pang of regret for the relatively easy life she had lived under Ada's patronage, and sighed at the thought of the pretty underwear that she had hardly worn, but she truly felt that Ada would understand. She had written to tell her the news but as yet had received no reply. But there was a letter waiting for her from Alfred in Gallipoli.

'Conditions are beyond my worst nightmares. We are entrenched here, just as they are on the Western Front. Whoever dreamt up such hideous warfare? I won't upset you by describing too much, but more men are succumbing to dysentery than being shot or shelled. There is talk of withdrawing. I hope to God we do.
I can't believe you want to go to France. The nurses and VADs are here too of course, mostly on Hospital ships, Bless their courageous hearts. I fear for you Lyddy,
but thank God for you and all the plucky, brave girls that do it.'

Finally, just after Christmas in January 1916 - she and Hermione packed their uniforms, rubber boots and sou`westers and embarked for `somewhere across the channel`.

Lydia supressed her disappointment that it wasn`t to be the Dardanelles. All the same, for some unaccountable reason, Lydia packed some of her pretty underwear along with her flannel drawers and thick undervests.

*

"Oh, my God, I didn`t expect it to be like this!" Lydia murmured to Hermione who looked just as terrified as she felt. They were on board old London buses painted grey, travelling through the blighted French countryside, after a miserable channel crossing which they had spent retching over the side.

"I didn`t think the war had reached this far," Hermione said, as they passed shattered, ruined villages.

The hospital, about thirty miles from Calais was a converted chateau and inside the main ward – probably what used to be the main living quarters, there were beds for about fifty men. Various large rooms, which had once been witness to luxurious living, were now given over to operating theatres, sluice rooms, storage spaces and offices. Upstairs, they were told, were housed the patients who were `very disturbed.` Lydia knew that many suffered from something called shell-shock, and from the screams and cries in the night, she wondered if these men would ever be normal again.

Their quarters were housed in the old stables that had been converted into small sleeping cubicles. There was a small basin every five cubicles, for washing, and the latrines were at the end.

The wounded were brought in a steady stream – initially by train, then ambulance. They were meant to receive the cases that could be patched up and sent back to the trenches. Sometimes the wounded were everywhere including the courtyard. Lizzie had been right; it was beyond anything she could have imagined. Some of the men had been saved from amputation by a new treatment of irrigating bad wounds with hypochlorus acid solution. This reduced the onset of sepsis and gangrene, but the men hated the painful process. Within a few days Lydia was carrying out this treatment, and the soldiers seemed to tolerate it better when she did it, for she talked to them, often telling them stories about home and amusing anecdotes about the schoolchildren. It soothed her as much as them, for she had to have other pictures in her mind other than what she saw before her

They worked tirelessly day after day with little sleep. The operating theatre worked round the clock, and many men could not be saved. Lydia thought she would never get used to the agonies of the dying; the young boys crying out for their mothers, their pain and torment only relieved by morphine. Their screams haunted her dreams during the little sleep she managed to snatch.

In the middle of this living hell she received a letter from Jack, months old. He apologised for not writing sooner.

`... *but I'm not sure you want to hear the truth – how the heat and the flies are driving us all mad.*

Thank God for the times of withdrawal from the front. I love to bathe in the sea which is like a warm bath compared

160

to the chill of the River Severn! There are many men from Australia and New Zealand come all this way to fight for the Mother Country, and what brave lads they are. But so many destined for an early grave in this God-forsaken land.

When I knew we were coming to this part of the world, I remembered the poetry of Byron. What is happening here and in France would surely inspire different words. There is no romance and grandeur about this war. I was a fool to think there ever was.

Sorry Lyddy, but poetry is very hard to write.

Except, I am yours, Always and forever, Jack

Lydia wept, hoping he was still alive, for they had received the news that the British had finally withdrawn from the Dardanelles. As usual, she finally fell into an exhausted, dreamless sleep for four short hours before she had to once more carry out her duties.

*

She eventually heard from Alfred that their regiment had been evacuated from the beaches in the previous September, when Jack had been slightly wounded by shrapnel and Alfred had succumbed to the effects of dysentery. Jack was taken by hospital ship to Malta and remained in a military hospital for several weeks. Alfred recovered well enough to be sent back to Blighty from where he had written to Lydia.

'I shall be joining my regiment in Flanders next week. Jack is recovering well in a Convalescent Home in Leamington, where I visited him last week. He promises to write. I have had leave at home with Ma and Pa of course. Ma has softened towards you a great deal, but Pa will not have your name mentioned in the house and forbids Ma to

161

write. Oh, Lyddy I do hope you will think it has all been worth it.`

Lydia had just been holding tightly onto a young Tommy`s hand, comforting him as he lay dying, thinking she was his mother.

"Yes. It`s worth it," she said quietly to herself.

*

In March she finally received an up to date letter from Jack. No poetry now, and it chilled Lydia to sense how changed he seemed. She knew it was hardly surprising, witnessing what he had.

`My little lady – will you ever be mine? Shall we even see each other again? It was the image of your dear face that kept me going, that still gives me hope. Yes I have hope again at last, for a while it deserted me. Indeed, even words deserted me. I am so sorry, for your words, your little stories and cheerful anecdotes cheered me at times. I'm not doing very well now, am I? But I know you deserved to hear that I am recovering. I am in Plymouth and shall soon be well enough to join my regiment in France. Father has tried to pull strings to get me out of it, but I need to go. In some perverse way I miss it. The stoic bravery of the men – so many gone now. I saw a lot of Alfred And I miss him too – such a revelation, such a good officer – soon promoted To lieutenant! You Winters are made of strong stuff, eh?*

I wonder when we shall meet again?

Til then, I am yours, Always and forever – Jack.

*

She later received another short missive from him saying he was in Plymouth for more training. Lydia was determined to move heaven and earth to see him, and eventually Matron consented to her taking a few days leave in late April. She crossed the channel again, hardly able to contain her excitement. They were to meet at last.

As she sat waiting for him in the lounge of the Royal Hotel, vainly attempting to read, she sensed his presence before she turned to see him; tall and handsome as ever, in his sub-lieutenant's uniform. He took her in his arms, and he held her so tightly, she could hardly breath, but she never wanted him to let her go. When he finally released her, they smiled as they touched each other's cheeks, both wet with tears. Their surroundings, indeed, the world retreated as they gazed at each other, silently reaffirming their love for each other; their meeting of souls. Still cupping her face he kissed her gently on the lips.

"Oh, Jack! Your moustache tickles," Lydia touched his mouth gently. "But, my, it does suit you."

They sat down, both feeling a little shy with each other.

"How fine you look in your uniform, I hope I didn`t get you into trouble sending the note, I didn`t know how else to …" as she prattled on, Lydia realised that Jack still hadn`t spoken. He seemed transfixed by her, and as she took in the look of him, she noticed the tiny lines of suffering around his mouth, but he was still her Jack. He took one of her hands and examined it in wonder.

"My hands are a trifle rough and work-worn I`m afraid, all that carbolic and disinfectant …"

"You`ve cut your hair." His voice was thick with emotion.

She touched her bobbed hair. "It`s so much easier, the lice – but then you`ll know…"

163

"Yes, I know. What are you reading?"

"A collection of poems by Christina Rosetti. You used to love poetry, Jack…"

He waved the book away dismissively. "If it pleases you. Come, let`s go for a walk. It`s a pleasant evening."

They walked and Lydia, to relieve the tension she felt emanating from her darling Jack, chatted on about the few ways the nurses tried to bring cheer to the patients, and themselves. How they occasionally performed small concerts for the men – amazingly at Christmas someone had even commandeered a piano. Jack told her about his bleak little Christmas at Leamington, and of how he had no intention of ever going back there. Suddenly he turned to her and said; "marry me Lydia!"

"But Jack, I need my parent`s permission, I`m under twenty one!"

"You forged your birth certificate didn`t you? Marry me. It`s war time, the usual restrictions no longer apply. Tomorrow, I`ll see the padre!"

"Oh Jack, oh, yes!"

Jack picked Lydia up and swung her round. Once more he was her carefree, jolly boy. The wind whipped her hair into her eyes and she threw back her head and laughed. This was the happiest day of her life. Nothing could spoil things now, surely?

Twenty

But once again Lydia`s joy was to be short lived. She knew something was wrong the minute Jack walked into the lounge of the hotel the following morning.

"I – I don`t know how to tell you …we`ll have to wait…my embarkation has come through. I have to leave in two hours."

He led her to a corner tucked away from the main room where they held each other, Lydia fighting back the tears. "We`ll find another time, there will be another time, won't there Jack?"

"Of course, oh, yes my little lady! Look, I`ve been saving this for you."

He handed her a small box. Lydia opened it to reveal a sapphire and diamond ring. Jack took it out and slipped it onto her engagement finger.

"There! It fits! You are my betrothed, my beloved!" They embraced, and Jack kissed away Lydia`s tears. "Oh, God I want you so! If only we could be alone…after everything that`s happened …come to my room Lydia, please!"

"Oh, Jack, you know I love you, I want you too my dearest, but…well, we`ve waited so long…" she looked down at her ring.

"You asked if there would be another time – and why? Because like me you know that everything is so uncertain – so many subalterns like me killed – our life expectancy is …"

Lydia touched his lips. "Don`t say it Jack. I know. But you will survive, I know you will, and knowing I am waiting – that`s what will keep you alive, that`s what will protect you."

Jack smiled at her blind faith, her naivety. As he smoothed back her hair he said, "You are a wonder little lady. This path you have pursued, your faith in me, your love – I do hope it has been worth it."

"Oh yes, Jack, of course, and it all makes me feel closer to you."

They sat quietly in their secluded corner, and Lydia thought to herself that it had been worth every agonizing second of the mud, blood, tears – the waiting and not knowing - just to be spending these few precious hours with her beloved.

Later, they walked on the Hoe, and found a seat looking out to sea. Taking Lydia`s hand Jack said, "if we had married as I had intended, you would be my beneficiary, my next of kin. I can`t leave you knowing that if anything happened to me, that you would have to exist on your pitiful VAD allowance. I know Ada has been generous, but she too is in a perpetual state of danger. I want something certain in your life." Jack explained that he had opened a modest account for her, and promised to send a small allowance every month. "Hopefully it won't be long until everything I have is yours."

He kissed away her tears and they clung to each other until Jack had to finally tear himself away.

Back in France, Lydia and Hermione were transferred to a larger hospital near Rienne, where huge marquee style tents had been added to house the wounded, who still arrived daily, and the remorseless toil of tending to their awful wounds continued.

Lydia heard from Alfred occasionally. He was near Ypres, where he wrote sparingly of the conditions in the trenches of the salient being beyond belief, with the mud, relentless shelling and poor condition of his men.

Jack wrote to say his battalion was occupying the rear trenches around Albert.

Everyone knew that this was going to be `the big push`. Countless divisions were entrenched along the Somme. Artillery fire began at the end of June and continued for eight continuous, nerve shattering days. The bombardment was meant to destroy much of the opposing defences and cut the wires, making it easy for the infantry to take the front trenches, and crush the German lines of defence. Instead, the heavy barrage gave the enemy good warning. When the first wave walked in slow formation over the top on the sunny morning of July 1st, they were systematically mown down by the German machine guns. The few that reached the wires found that they had not been cut. The slaughter continued unabated, as wave after wave of men were mown down. Many fell back into the trenches before they could leave them. 57,000 men died that bloody day, for virtually no ground gained. Many lay rotting in the sun in no-man`s-land.

Jack`s battalion had been in the reserve trenches and had not been called upon to walk into death that day. There was much work to be done re-stocking the communication trenches, and bringing up ammunition. Two weeks later they were part of an attack further up the line at Bazentin. Minutes into the attack, Jack had been blown into a shell hole. He recovered consciousness hours later, and found himself next to his sergeant whose face was half missing, and his chest a bloody mess. Under the cover of darkness, he crawled back to his own trench, dragging Watts, his sergeant with him. He couldn't bear the thought of the rats getting to him. Half the battalion had been killed that day, and except for a bruised forehead, Jack was unharmed. The wood they had attempted to take was still in enemy hands.

Jack led a couple of night raids into the enemy trenches, where he experienced hand to hand fighting and on one occasion drove the Germans out of their trench, capturing three of them. But they had to return to their own line when there was no back up. The stalemate continued, but Lydia was overjoyed to receive a letter from Jack, telling her of these events, albeit weeks later.

*

"Hermione! I can't believe it!" Lydia and her friend had excitedly collected their post that morning and were grabbing a few precious moments with a mug of weak tea in the crumbling basement kitchen of the hospital. "Alfred is taking leave next week, and thinks Jack can join him in Boulogne. He wants me to go too!"

"Then you must, I'm sure Matron will allow it, you're overdue leave."

Both girls were worn out - most of the staff in the hospital were, but lately Lydia was finding it harder and harder to drag herself from her bed. It had been intolerably hot and she had succumbed to a bout of influenza the previous month. When she saw the matron later in the day, she unreservedly gave her permission.

"In fact, I think you should go home for at least a month, or you`ll end up in hospital yourself."

*

Alfred – now Captain Winters, had booked rooms for them all at the Folkestone Hotel, Boulogne. He was there to greet Lydia, and she was shocked at the change in him. The boy was now undoubtedly a man, he stood tall and proud with his thick moustache and impeccable uniform – but his hand trembled as he lit a cigarette after hugging her, and there were lines around his mouth and eyes that hadn`t been there before. His haunted eyes, a paler version of her own, regarded his sister with grave concern.

"Lyddy you look ill. God knows I have to be here, but you – haven`t you done enough?"

"How much is enough, Alfred?" She wondered at his concern for her, when he looked so worn out himself.

"Ah, that is the question we would all like answered. Go home Lydia. I`ll write to mother, she should know – father will take you in, he has to."

"There you are, my two favourite people in all the world!" Jack, now Lieutenant Albright, embraced them both. After a few words of greeting, Alfred left the lovers alone.

"You look well, Jack, I knew you would come back to me," said Lydia squeezing his hand.

"Lucky so far eh?" He led Lydia to a quiet corner, and for a while they needed no words, as Lydia lay against his shoulder. Eventually he said. "Can`t get used to the quiet. It`s the incessant bombardments, the shelling that gets to you. And yet you know, just occasionally, some of those `star` shells, as they light

169

up the sky have a kind of beauty. I know it sounds crazy, but one night, on watch as a lone shell burst in the sky, it made me think of that night in the garden in the rain."

"It seems like another lifetime …"

"I know I don`t quote poetry any more, but you know, that night even no-man`s land seemed at peace, and I remembered –

`As often through the purple night
Below the starry clusters bright
Some bearded meteor trailing light
Moves over still Shalott.`

Ridiculous, of course. No-man`s land - Shalott! Ah, well, a poem from a time when warriors were knights and ladies sat at their weaving. How could anyone have ever imagined how the warriors of today would blow each other apart?"

"Don`t Jack."

"No, it doesn`t do does it? But looking at you my little lady! Those dark circles under your eyes – methinks a spot of weaving would do you good."

She looked deeply into his eyes. "You do me good Jack. Only you. Tonight… I know how you have wanted me in the past…" she fought to find the right words. "How long can we tempt fate Jack? I`ve been such a puritanical fool. I love you, come to me tonight…" She hugged him to hide her blushing face.

"Lovely Lydia," Jack murmured at last. He held her flushed face and kissed her eyes, wet with tears.

In her room later, Lydia bathed and wore her beloved silk undergarments beneath her uniform. Her head throbbed and she had no need to pinch her cheeks, as her colour was extremely flushed. "Please

170

God don`t let me be ill, tonight of all nights" she said into her mirror.

But at dinner with Alfred and Jack, she could barely eat at all, and the room began to swim. She collapsed as she rose to leave the table.

A doctor diagnosed exhaustion, and advised bed rest for at least a week.

Jack stayed with her for the two days left of his leave, during which she drifted in and out of consciousness. During one brief coherent moment she said with tears in her eyes "I thought that this time…this time we could really be together… you know, like you wanted last time. I`m so sorry I didn`t then…"

"It`s alright my darling. Just like you said, knowing you are waiting keeps me safe."

"I brought such pretty things for you to see me in."

"Save them. We have so much to look forward to."

Jack kissed her goodbye and a nurse was engaged to stay with her. Alfred was able to remain until she began to recover a day later.

"You must go back to England Lyddy. I've written to mother and she says you will be welcome back at School House. She says father still finds it hard to forgive you, but …"

"No, Alfred. I am needed here. Give me another week …"

Before Alfred left however, a letter arrived from Ada.

`Jack has informed me of your illness. You must go home, at least for a while. I have stressed upon you time after time the need for respite of some kind. I myself have just returned to Flanders after a month back in London. If you will not go back to Claines, please avail yourself of my hospitality in your old room. Sylvia an old friend of yours is staying there so you will have company. When you are feeling better, you could offer your services at the Convalescent Home for Officers which has been opened nearby, as I know you will still want to serve in some way. `

Finally, Lydia agreed on this compromise, and a relieved Alfred left to re-join his regiment in Ypres.

Lydia once again crossed the channel for England, and this time when she knocked at the door of number 5, an almost benevolent Mrs. Harding was there to greet her. She succumbed to the comforts of the blue room once again – quite touched when Mrs. Harding told her that the room had been kept especially for her. Sylvia, a fellow nurse from France had returned to England the month before. She was currently `helping out` at the Convalescent Home in nearby Belgrave Square, and in the evenings the girls were glad of each other's company.

She received three more letters from Jack – all together, as so often happened – in late October – there had been more battles on the Somme - then nothing. As Christmas 1916 approached, she was cheered by the news that Asquith had resigned and Lloyd George became prime minister. She knew her father would be pleased, and said so in her letter to her mother, informing her that she was back in London.

On Christmas Eve Hermione appeared on the doorstep, and invited her to spend Christmas in Hampshire with her family, but Lydia stayed in Grosvenor Crescent and celebrated quietly with Mrs. Harding and Sylvia. She received Christmas greetings from her brother, but again, nothing from Jack.

*

Hermione returned in the new year, and persuaded Lydia to join her to a few tea parties and concerts - even a trip to the opera at Covent Garden, which left Lydia spell bound. She was surprised when her friend confided that she couldn't face returning to France. "I just can't believe this wretched war still drags on. I must do something, but as yet … I think I may return to the Royal London."

"I had thought of that myself," said Lydia. "But I am so worried about Jack. If I go back to Rienne, I may have a better chance of finding out what has happened to him."

"Please stay Lydia," Hermione begged. "We could always help at the Convalescent Home for Officers in the Square with Sylvia. It is better than nothing."

Lydia nodded. "Better than nothing will have to suffice. Ada did advise that and I know she is in a better position than me to find out things over there. She'll let me know of any news."

Lydia wrote to Ada and received an unusually prompt reply, saying that she would make enquiries.

Within the week both girls were welcomed with open arms at the annexe to King Edward V11's Hospital for Officers, where the conditions and atmosphere was very genteel and organised. Most of the men were in the final stages of recovery, although some had sustained dreadful wounds; many had lost limbs and many had been blinded. She and Hermione were soon in the old routine of changing beds, dressing, and writing letters for the blind. They were kept busy, but the work bore no resemblance whatsoever to the primitive conditions and relentless death toll of the Field Hospitals.

One afternoon Lydia was requested by a young blind Lieutenant to read from his favourite book, Dickens' Tale of Two Cities, and within minutes several other officers gathered to listen. This became a regular part of her daily routine – reading for an appreciative audience, and other young men soon added their own requests.

In late February she visited her bank to withdraw a little money, and was summoned to see the Bank Manager who told her that the monthly regular deposits had ceased the month before. Oh, Jack! Lydia left the bank in a trance. She had heard nothing more from Ada or Alfred – she felt at her wits end with worry.

"If anything – bad – has happened to him no-one would notify me. What am I to do?" she confided in Hermione.

"Write to his next of kin of course – his father, the Honourable Sir Francis Albright at the House of Commons."

"Hermione, you are a genius!"

So Lydia wrote, candidly explaining her relationship to Jack, and saying how desperate she was for news of him.

She had not heard a thing by April, but there was good news that America had entered the war, which again was offset by reports of the heavy death toll at the battle of Arras.

Then out of the blue, at the beginning of June, Lydia walked into the drawing room after a stint at the home to find Ada stretched out on the Chesterfield, snoring softly.

Twenty One

"An old army friend was coming home on leave so grabbed the chance of a lift to Boulogne," Ada told Lydia the following day. "Taking my own advice; time to recharge the old batteries! By the way, any news of Jack?"

"Nothing yet" said Lydia, and she told her of her letter to Francis Albright.

"Mmm. I think it`s time I paid a visit to my dear uncle."

This proved to be unnecessary however, as the following morning Lydia received an envelope bearing the House of Commons insignia. She opened it with an overwhelming mixture of foreboding and excitement.

Dear Miss Winters,

In reply to your enquiry regarding my son, Jack Albright, I regret to inform you that he was posted missing, presumed dead in October last during a battle at the Transloy Ridges on the River Somme. Consequently as executor of his estate, the small monthly allowance Jack arranged for you to receive has been curtailed. I am aware that Jack was fond of you, but any union between you would have been impossible. I recall that you have family in Worcestershire where you held a position as a school teacher. My advice would be to return to your family and resume your previous life.

I wish you well,

Lydia was stunned; Jack missing, presumed dead! The dark fear, that hard nugget of dread that had gnarled away at her insides for months threatened to disgorge and choke her. Missing! Everyone knew what missing meant. It meant that no body parts could be found. The shells simply blew men to smithereens. She ran to the blue room, passing Ada on the stairs. She thrust the letter at her, locked the door and wept until she could weep no more. She refused all food and drink that Ada sent up to her, and stayed there all the following day. She was totally inconsolable.

"She needs time of course. I'm afraid I'm totally useless with soothing words, I'm a person of action, and shortly that will be Lydia's salvation. In the meantime gals, I am leaving her to you," Ada told Hermione and Sylvia. Astonishingly, she seemed totally restored, resuming her rounds of meetings and lobbying the rich and powerful.

Lydia shut herself away and mourned, refusing to see anyone. She read and re-read every word of every poem and letter Jack had ever sent. Eventually she locked them away, fearing they would disintegrate with the constant soaking of her tears. She tried to find comfort in her poetry and re-read The Lady of Shalott. The poem would always resonate with her. She had even thought her life in some ways mirrored the Lady's story. Lydia had lived a sheltered life protected from the world and had found her destiny with her own Sir Lancelot. Is this the price she had to pay for daring to look at Camelot? In the poem, the lady pays the ultimate price, but in life it is Jack. Oh, it was unbearable!

Eventually it was Hermione who coaxed her out of her room, and within hours Lydia began to rail against Jack's father.

"The arrogance of that man Francis Albright! It implies that all I was worried about was the allowance! I don`t give a fig about the money anyway. I can earn my own, and will! And what about `any union between us would have been impossible`? Oh, I can`t bear it! We`ll never be able to prove our love to the world now."

"Well at least you`re getting your fighting spirit back. You have to carry on. I know it`s terrible, but what choice do you have?"

Lydia considered for a moment. "I have a choice. I`m going back to France. I`ll be of more use there. I need to be where Jack was, close to the poor devils who are picked up off the battlefield. I`m going to give my notice tomorrow."

Ada was pleased to see Lydia up and about and took her out to tea at the Savoy. Lydia knew that she found it difficult to show her feelings, but at one point she took her hand, and staring at the cake stand said "You and Jack would have made a go at it, I`m sure. But he`s made the ultimate sacrifice like so many thousands of our brave boys." She screwed her eyes shut for a moment. "We simply have to believe it is for a greater cause, although many of us find it hard…" she faltered, then seemed to gather strength; "Jack would want you to focus on the future, as we all must. Hermione tells me you want to return to France, although…"

"Don`t try to stop me Ada! Look at you, you`ve served longer than anyone, and you`re returning soon."

"Yes, and although I now see the total waste and futility of it all, somehow, out there, in the thick of all the danger and mayhem, I feel as if my whole life has been preparing me for this. It is where I belong."

Lydia looked at her with admiration. She herself had been impulsive and out of her depth, but in her own small way she had been determined to help – and to be where Jack was. She had done it once and she could do it again.

However, two days later she received a letter to say that her services would not be required.

"There is no shortage of volunteers now, and your illness would have a bearing, especially as some sort of influenza is taking its toll on and off in the trenches," Hermione told her. "When Ada returns to Flanders, come back to the Convalescent Home, they'll welcome you with open arms."

Everyone in the know was aware of a third battle at Ypres in the offing, and Ada bade them farewell to rejoin her unit. Lydia picked up where she left off at the Home, combining her nursing duties with reading to the men most afternoons. But most of the time it felt as if she was sleepwalking through life; an essential part of her had been destroyed. What did it matter what she did now? Life had no real meaning for her.

*

One morning in late November, she opened the door of a recently arrived patient, carrying fresh dressings, and came face to face with Edwin Bengeworth.

"What the hell are you doing here?" he snarled.

Lydia had experienced aggression from patients in pain and confusion many times, but this was the first time she had known the patient personally; and Edwin Bengeworth of all people! She stepped back, saying to the Doctor in charge -"I'll get Nurse Templeton to assist…"

"You'll do no such thing" Dr. Staines insisted, "pull yourself together nurse."

He drew back the sheet, and Lydia could see that Edwin Bengeworth's left leg had been amputated above the knee, and there were livid scars reaching into his groin.

The sight of Edwin Bengeworth, this once proud, arrogant man, lying vulnerable and panic-stricken, shocked her to the core.

"Get out! Get that little whore away from me!" he screamed.

She backed away, aghast at the sight of Edwin thrashing about the bed, coughing and hurling profanities she had not heard since France.

"Alright, nurse! Send Nurse Templeton to assist," Dr. Staines shouted.

She was still trembling ten minutes later when Dr. Staines found her in the kitchen.

"He's calm now, I've given him an injection. Captain Bengeworth was obviously shocked to see you here. Whatever your personal connections..."

"There are no connections Doctor. Captain Bengeworth's father was the local Squire in the village where I lived." Lydia stood up. "Of course, I shall leave at once if that's what you want."

"I don't think that will be necessary, you have become a valued member of staff. We shall just have to ensure that your paths cross as little as possible."

Their paths did not cross until the following week. She led a blind Officer into the day room to a seat by the window.

"Describe the garden to me," he asked. In spite of the time of year, a weak sun was filtering through a gap in the clouds. Lydia described the green, luxuriant grass, and the lacy pattern of the trees against the sky.

"You make it sound poetical. My last sight was the stinking mud of Flanders," he said in a flat tone.

"Oh, I'm no poet. Do you like Wordsworth?" she asked.

He nodded.

At his request Lydia read Wordsworth's 'Intimations of Immortality'. When she reached verse 10, her voice broke with emotion;

Though nothing can bring back the hour
Of Splendour in the grass, of glory in the flower;
We will grieve not, rather find
Strength in what remains behind;

In the silence the lieutenant reached for her hand. "You've lost someone."

"Yes."

"Powerful words. They will sustain me for a while, perhaps they will do the same for you."

Lydia could do no more than squeeze his hand.

When she returned the book to its shelf later, Edwin was sitting in his bath chair nearby, scowling at her.

"Poetry! Damned nonsense. Think you're back at the village school do you?" he scoffed.

"Good day Captain Bengeworth," she said as politely as she could manage.

"Nurse! Get me out of here!" he called angrily, and Hermione came rushing in to wheel him out.

Ada was killed near Ypres, forever to be known as Passchendale. A stray shell had hit her make-shift

181

headquarters and Ada and several others had been killed instantly. Lydia thought she had no more tears, but she wept for her friend and mentor, a courageous woman who had achieved so much. Back at No.5 Mrs Harding was bereft.

"There was nobody like her. She was a real lady. Bloody war!"

Lydia sat quietly with her and Charters in the kitchen, wondering what they would all do without her. For now all she could do was to follow her advice, and simply carry on.

Two days later she came face to face with Edwin in the day room.

"Miss Winters, wait a moment."

She stood in front of him, half expecting an insult.

"I hear you've had bad news."

"Yes."

"I'm sorry."

"No you're not. In any case, everyone receives bad news sooner or later. It was my turn once again."

"Again? Not your brother I hope."

"No, not Alfred. A ...dear friend."

Edwin seemed to consider this for a moment.

"Was it that Albright fellow? I seem to remember him staying with your family that summer, before..."

"Before the world went mad? Yes, it was Jack Albright. We were engaged to be married."

Edwin did not attempt to conceal his surprise.

"Now if you'll excuse me..." Lydia began to walk away.

"Miss Winters!" She stopped. "Miss Winters, I know my behaviour has been appalling, and I apologise. The shock y`know, the shock of seeing you… of you seeing me like this…"

He began coughing into a handkerchief, stained pink, his whole body shaking with the effort. When the coughing subsided, she gently touched his shoulder.

"I know," she said softly, but knew better than to show pity.

"Would you like a short turn around the garden?" she asked briskly.

"Sure you can spare the time?" he sniffed.

"I have a few moments before I go off duty," Lydia replied.

*

Everyone did their best to make Christmas as pleasant as possible for the patients at the home. Lydia joined the choir for the Carol Service on Christmas Eve, and helped serve the Christmas Lunch, but returned to Grosvenor Crescent for Mrs. Harding`s Christmas pudding with Sylvia.

"We won't be able to stay here indefinitely now." Sylvia voiced what everyone was thinking. "Well I`m not going home with my tail between my legs, for my ma to say `I told you so`. It`s back to France for me."

"And I shall try again. I gave in too easily the last time!" said Lydia determinedly.

In February The Representation of the People Act was passed which gave the vote to property owning women over the age of thirty. The girls gathered to celebrate and raise a toast to Ada who had worked long and hard towards this goal. It was another cruel irony that she hadn`t lived to see it.

Then Hermione cheered them with the news that she would shortly be announcing her engagement, to an old family friend. Everything was changing, and it was to prove the same for Lydia in the news contained in the first ever letter from her mother.

Alfred had been wounded, and after hospitalisation on the south coast was currently in a Convalescent home in Battenhall, Worcester.

Your brother is desperate to see you. Please come home.

I'm sorry to say that your father remains implacable in his attitude, but we can make arrangements for you to stay at The Mug Inn.

"I shall leave tomorrow," she told Sylvia. "Poor, poor Alfred. I don`t know how badly wounded he is, but I can`t bear to think of losing him too. Oh, please God no! And to think that my father`s door remains closed against me. Well, I shall stay in a fine hotel, I still have savings!"

She bustled off for a final day at the Home, and later she pushed Edwin round the Square that evening – it had become a daily ritual, after he had joined some of the others listening to her readings, much to her surprise. She told him the news of Alfred.

"Sorry to hear it. Of course you must go. I hope you find him … well, you know…"

Lydia stopped and sat on a bench on the green. She looked at Edwin as he stared into space. Somehow, gradually over the past weeks they had formed a kind of friendship which neither of them would have thought possible. But then, the experiences of the past three years had changed them both beyond recognition.

"Why are you here, Edwin – in London, so far away from Worcester? Your family must find it difficult to visit," she said.

"Huh! They visited me in hospital a couple of times, at least father, mother and little Margaret did. Harriet is married now, lives in India with some wretched tea planter, well out of this shambles, anyway. My mother couldn't look me in the eye and snivelled all the time, Margaret stared at me like a startled hare, and father just complained about the estate falling to pieces, full of doom and gloom. When it came to convalescence, I insisted on coming here. How I can possibly fit back into their lives I can`t imagine."

"But you will I`m sure, in time."

The cynical sneer was still there. "Time, the healer of all things, eh? Ha! How can you possibly remain so hopeful? After all you were in the thick of it yourself in that bloody hospital."

Was she hopeful? "This war can`t go on forever. Things will never be the same for anyone, but you do still have your family. I am returning because my brother needs me. You may realise that you need your family, and given time they will want to do their best for you."

"Hmph, time. Don`t know that I've got much of that. I`m not bloody stupid, I know what the gas has done to my lungs."

"Then go home to the people who love you. They will adjust in time."

Edwin`s voice softened. "He`s a lucky fellow your brother. You know if he hadn`t needed you, I

185

might have asked you to be my nurse. Might have gone back to the Grange then."

Lydia looked away. "Dr. Staines will find you an excellent nurse I`m sure."

"If I do go home will you come and see me?"

"Yes of course."

She tucked the blanket around him and pushed him back to the Home, wondering why she had answered so quickly, and if she could possibly keep her promise.

Twenty Two

"Captain Winters suffered a bad shrapnel shoulder wound, which became infected. It is healing slowly, but we don't know if he will ever regain full use of his arm," Matron explained to Lydia at the Convalescent Home. "You will find him changed. He is suffering from neurasthenia. You see when the soldiers spent so long at the front, the incessant noise of the shells …"

"Yes, I know." Lydia told her she had nursed in France. So that's what they're calling it now, she thought. My poor brother is suffering from shell shock.

Alfred was propped up in bed, and stared at her incomprehensively when she entered the room. Lydia was dismayed to see that it was his right arm that was injured. She sat next to him quietly and took his other trembling hand, gently raising it to her lips.

"Lyddy?" he whispered hoarsely, and a tear trickled down his cheek.

"I'm here, it's alright now Alfred," Lydia murmured, stroking his clammy forehead until he fell asleep. She felt as if nothing would ever be 'alright' again, but she would do everything in her power to help her dear brother.

As she closed the door to his room, she turned to see her mother and father walking towards her. For a split second she was transfixed, but then all she could think was; here is my dear mother; my mother!

"Mama!" she cried, and she threw her arms around her.

Eliza responded by hugging Lydia, who held onto her as if she would never let go. "Now Lydia dear, come, come."

As Lydia stepped back, still holding her mother`s hand, she saw her father had taken a seat nearby obviously embarrassed by this show of affection. Eliza blinked away a tear and extended her free hand towards her husband.

"Lydia." He stood up slowly appraising her, ignoring Eliza`s hand. "Quite the lady. We are all glad that you could find time to visit your brother. How is he today?"

Well, at least her father was speaking to her; but he was so distant. It was as if she were a stranger.

"He …he said my name… oh, the poor boy's nerves are shattered, but I have seen worse cases and seen great improvements …"

"Yes, of course. Your hospital work," Henry interrupted. "I shall never understand to this day what drove you to take such a foolhardy course, but seeing you now … well, I am very relieved that you appear unscathed. Indeed, you look quite prosperous."

"Yes, well that`s thanks to Ada, Jack Albright`s cousin, she rather took me under her wing."

"Hmph, you`re lucky some-one did. Now why don`t you walk with your mother in the garden, I`m sure you have plenty to catch up on. I`ll sit and read the newspaper until Alfred wakes up."

Lydia took her mother`s arm, and they walked in the grounds.

"Oh ma, I can`t believe it! Sometimes I thought I`d never see you again – and papa, do you think he`ll ever forgive me? Have you?"

"My dear girl, my darling daughter! " Eliza`s voice broke with emotion as she patted her hand. "It was quite a shock seeing you here today, so unexpected! But at least it meant your father couldn`t ignore you. He`s a very proud man. But it`s a start. It will take time. As with Alfred, it will all take time."

"I am not the impulsive child that ran away two years ago, although I have absolutely no regrets mother. So much has happened ..." Lydia fought against the instinct to tell her mother everything, but all that mattered now was Alfred. "Oh Ma! It`s not just the wounds you can see..."

"Yes, his nerves, Lydia! He didn`t recognise us for days, and he doesn`t walk properly – the doctor says there is no reason why he shouldn`t, but he just trembles and collapses ... and apparently he has terrible nightmares."

"I`m going to stay and try to help. I stayed in a small Inn in Sidbury last night, but Matron has recommend lodgings nearby."

"But how can you afford all this? And your clothes, so stylish..."

"Ada was very good to me, treated me like her niece. In return I helped with her organisations and voluntary work. I have saved a little money and my VAD wages ..."

"I really should write and thank her."

"I`m afraid Ada was killed in Flanders a few weeks ago." Lydia took a deep breath and fingered the locket around her neck, "and Jack... he was

189

posted missing in October. We were engaged to be married. He gave me this ring." She held out her trembling hand to her mother

Eliza was speechless.

"We met briefly twice, in Plymouth and Boulogne, but we have written to each other constantly, at least we did until …"

Eliza took her hand, and mother and daughter sat quietly, both too overwhelmed with emotion to speak. Eventually Henry called to tell them that Alfred was awake.

Once the Home knew of her VAD and nursing experience, Lydia was allowed to stay most of the day with Alfred. As a consequence he began to recover. Within days he was taking tentative steps within his room; and he was soon able to walk outside with an orderly and Lydia supporting him. Lydia coaxed and cajoled, just as she had with the children in her class and some of the wounded soldiers in her care. With sheer doggedness and perseverance she drove him on; often singing nursery rhymes and music hall songs, to create a rhythm for him to move to. Somehow, they worked through the invisible barrier that his mind had created, and vestiges of the old Alfred began to emerge. A few weeks later, it was decided that he could be discharged into Lydia's care.

They rented a small cottage in Slip Lane near the river, just as winter began to turn to spring. Lydia hid the newspapers which carried stories of the fear of a new German onslaught on the Western Front. She bought bicycles and they cycled around the country lanes or walked beside the river. Whilst walking or just sitting together in the twilight, they talked. Alfred spoke little about his time in the trenches – he relived that over and over again in his nightmares. Mostly they talked about their childhood and shared experiences. Then, one night, quite out of the blue, Alfred talked in great detail about Jack. It was as if he had forgotten the relationship between Jack and his sister, but Lydia didn't mind.

"He was from a different world of course; all those upper class young men with the world at their feet. Jack befriended me because I was clever; he used to crib my ideas. He was only interested in having a good time – no real interest in the law, yet he would probably have walked into one of the most prestigious law firms in London. But he took to me for some reason, and you know, I sort of worshipped him Lydia, because he was so generous and full of fun. He drew me out, made me feel I could aspire to being someone; he knew I would have to survive in their world if I was to become a lawyer. They accepted me because of Jack; and I just relished Jack's company and I know he liked me, he said he liked my 'quiet wisdom', whatever that is! When he said he wanted to go walking with me, to visit my home… Oh God! I was scared to death, afraid he would suddenly become aware of the gap between us, that he would mock me, my family, everything I held dear, even you, Lyddy… oh, of course you know Lyddy don't you?"

She nodded silently. Tears had been coursing down her cheeks during Alfred's monologue. Of course, Alfred loved him too, and his recollections had made Jack feel so close again, for she had been desperately trying to keep him locked up with her letters and memories. But now she found herself in a different place; being able to share Jack with Alfred.

"Four years ago – it seems like a lifetime. I was so young, so naïve, and yet I loved Jack from the moment I saw him, standing next to you at the top of the garden that sunny summer day. And he loved me too, I'm sure of it."

"Yes, sis of course he did, even though I doubted him at first. The last time we saw him, when you were feverish, he was beside himself with worry. I thought he would go AWOL, he was so afraid for you. He probably would have done if I hadn't been there. He made me swear to send you home. He wouldn't leave your bedside until the last minute. No doubt about it, Sis you were made for each other in spite of everything conspiring to keep you apart, first social convention then this bloody war…"

"All that concealment and pretence. Such a waste – and yet, if Jack were to walk in now, nothing could keep us apart. No-one would dare." Lydia clutched the locket round her neck and kissed it.

Jack walking back into her life. It was a tiny, secret vision that she constantly thought of, based on a hope or a dream that no effort could erase. Her reason told her that it was an impossible hope or dream, but she kept the vision deep inside her all the same, telling no-one, not even Alfred.

*

They visited their parents frequently, and it was good to see old friends and neighbours again. But the shadow of the war hung over every conversation; others had loved ones who were missing or killed,

192

and saddest of all was seeing the change in Taffy Jones. His son Tudor had eventually joined up and had been shot by a sniper on his first day in the trenches. Taffy still laboured at his forge, although the demand for horse shoes was diminishing. He merely nodded at Lydia. Apparently he hadn`t spoken since he had received news of his son`s death.

Will Shawcroft was still with his regiment in France, but they visited Lottie who was now engaged to a mutual friend who had joined the navy. Lizzie had returned from France and was now nursing again at the Royal Infirmary in Worcester. She too was engaged – to a pleasant young orthopaedic surgeon, and Lydia and Alfred had dinner with them on two occasions. Gradually Alfred was gaining in confidence, physically and socially. Then, out of the blue came an invitation from The Grange.

"My God, Lyddy! Edwin Bengeworth must be home – he`s inviting us to dinner!"

"Well that`s marvellous news – the fact that he`s decided to come home, I mean." She had told Alfred about her experience with him at the home, and his reluctance to return to Claines. She remembered her promise. "Mmm, I suppose we should go?"

*

It was a sombre affair. They were greeted by Sir Frederick who looked genuinely pleased to see them. He led them to the Drawing Room where Lady Amelia was seated alone.

"We wanted to thank you for all you did for Edwin," she said, shaking Lydia`s hand.

"But I was only doing my job, Lady Amelia"

"Edwin has said very little about ... about anything, but he has spoken of you. He said you were his Angel of Mercy."

Lydia and Alfred exchanged glances. "That doesn't sound much like Edwin," she said wryly.

"No, but then we seem to have lost most of the old Edwin. He can still be as belligerent as ever, but these days he's more thoughtful, and I have to say, totally undemanding, considering his ... illness. He reads a lot."

"That's how he came to tell us about you," said Sir Frederick "He said you used to read to him, and escaping into another world helped him forget this one. Anyway, when he knew you and Alfred were back in the district, he thought it would be jolly nice to see you again."

They moved into the cavernous dining room. Lydia could see the dividing doors across one side, and remembered that this was half of the ballroom where Edwin had held his summer ball. She caught her breath and her stomach clenched at the memory. She had been so in awe of the occasion, so impetuous, so in love with Jack.

Eventually Edwin joined them, limping slowly in with a heavy walking stick. He looked ashen faced and drawn. She couldn't help recalling the handsome imperious man of four years ago hosting his summer ball. He nodded shyly to Lydia and shook Alfred's hand.

"Your arm and my leg – together we might make a whole one, eh Alfred?"

He forced a laugh, that sparked off a spasm of coughing.

Eventually they settled down to eat in silence. After the soup Lydia quietly expressed her pleasure at the news that he was riding again.

"Hmph. Father told you did he? Well, I've managed a trot or two round the paddock, but I think it will be a while before I'll be riding to hounds. How about you Alfred? Never rode did you? What are your plans?"

"My arm will never be the same again, they tell me. Depends on whether I can strengthen my trigger finger."

"My God, so you might go back?" Edwin was incredulous.

"I see the medical board next month."

They all sat in silence as the maids served their meal. Lydia couldn't help thinking that some of the old Edwin very much in evidence, and somehow she was glad. She knew that his proud, high-handed manner was his defence against the world, and he would need it.

After dinner Sir Frederick and Lady Amelia took their leave, and Edwin led them to his den for coffee.

Edwin's den was the library, and he drank far more brandy than coffee.

"We all used to look forward to your sister reading to us at the hospital, Alfred. Grown men sitting round like infants in the school room …"

Alfred shot a glance at Lydia. "Steady on now, Edwin …"

After another bout of virulent coughing Edwin picked up a slim volume from the table. "Take no notice, didn't mean to insult the lady." He turned towards Lydia, looking at her properly for the first time during the whole evening.

"I'm sorry Lydia; I mean no disrespect – just can't help being bitter. Bitter and angry about the war, this wretched lung disease that is killing me slowly. Can't help thinking those men who were despatched quickly were the lucky ones. Remember the summer ball you came to? Half of the chaps there are dead now, the lucky ones. Remember old Horace who had a piggy back race with Kate on his back? Came back with half his face missing. Wears a metal plate over it now so as not to frighten the servants. That's when I count my blessings. Hah!"

Edwin stared into space for a long time, his eyes blurred with tears. Lydia and Alfred were lost in their own thoughts too, both seeing the long ago fairy tale vision of the summer ball. Eventually Edwin picked up a small book from the table at his side.

"Anyway, I wanted you to see this. It's a volume of poetry by Siegfred Sassoon. Yes, poetry, and the difference is, he's writing the truth, and it helps. Oh, God, yes it helps to think at last there's a voice to express what so many of us feel. A lot of the poems are a bit airy-fairy, but the ones about the war are more truthful than anything you'll read in the newspapers." He handed her the book entitled 'The Old Huntsman'.

Lydia arched an eyebrow. "Would you like me to read, or would you prefer the school room?"

"Touché," Edwin smiled, his look softening. "No take it home and read it. Come back and see me, and I'll enjoy talking about it with you." His features hardened again as he raised his chin. "Sorry I can`t see you out."

On the walk home Alfred asked if she would go and see Edwin again.

"Yes, why not?"

"Don`t befriend him out of pity Lydia. I know how the war has changed him, of course, but I can`t help remembering how he used to lust after you in the old days. Be careful, Liddy. Like so many of us his mind as well as his body is damaged."

"Yes, he used to be so powerful and intimidating, and he frightened me a little. But I've grown up a bit since then. Don`t worry Alfred, we can be no more than friends, you see the shell destroyed more than his leg. And his lungs – well he may only have a few years, and if I can be his friend and help a little, then I will. I assure you it`s not a relationship based on pity."

Lydia using the term relationship unnerved Alfred a little, but any further discourse was curtailed, as, in the gathering dusk, he could see Freddie and Polly walking towards them. Polly had seen them and was ushering Freddie across the road. Was she avoiding them?

Twenty Three

Alfred called out a greeting to them.

"Oh, it`s you. Can`t be too careful at this time of night," said Polly.

Lydia greeted them fondly and Freddie was so overcome with emotion that he could hardly speak.

"I think he thought he`d never see you again, Miss," smirked Polly. "So what was it like, out there in them `ospitals? Was it worth it?"

"It was pretty awful, just as you predicted. I just did my best…"

"I think there are a lot of soldiers alive today who think it was worth it Polly," Alfred said.

"Bloody war! You ask Taffy Jones if it was worth it. And `ave you seen poor John Stepford, used to work at the Grange with me sister? Came back a bloody wreck, minus `alf `is arm and `alf `is mind. You might `ave seen `im. Wanders up and down the lanes, beggin` from farm to farm like a tramp, and John Amphlett `is mate lyin` in pieces in the mud out there."

Alfred sighed deeply. "I know Polly, I was there, it was beyond imagination. When I said it was worth it, I meant it was worth saving those who could be saved, and if it hadn`t been for the brave nurses and doctors out there many more would have died."

"I know you`re angry Polly. I know you lost Hal." Lydia reached out and touched her arm. She nodded and sniffed.

Freddie spoke at last. "You`m looking well Mr. Alfred. One of the lucky ones eh?

"Is that it then, out of the army for good now?" said Polly.

"I have to see the medical board next week actually. I'm feeling fit as a fiddle, so no doubt I'll be back at the front again soon."

"Oh, l-let's hope not Master Alfred," Freddie managed to say at last.

Lydia knew that it could happen, they were still so desperate for good men – for any men. Alfred had given so much, she would pray for a miracle. He had indeed recovered very well, but they both knew a posting back on the front lines would finish him. "We hope it won't come to that" she murmured.

They bade the couple farewell, and walked on in silence for a while, then Alfred remarked how sad it was that they had never had children.

"Yes, having babies might have softened Polly, for she seems to carry a bit of a grudge against the world, even before she lost Hal."

"Is it against the world, or just you?" teased Alfred. "She always thought poor old Freddie carried a torch for you, and he did look rather overwhelmed, seeing you."

"Oh, don't be ridiculous Alfred." Polly hated her because she had covered up Aggie's crime, but she had never told Alfred. It was a secret she would take to her grave.

Alfred stopped and took his sister's hand. "You always did underestimate your effect on people, and it's not just your beauty. I meant it when I said that to Polly about the men in hospital."

"Oh Alfred, sometimes I wonder if I was any use at all – you know what it was like, the cries, the smells, the endless streams of bleeding, mangled bodies. Polly was right – I was just being selfish. All

I wanted was to find Jack. And I didn`t Alfred, I failed in everything!"

"But you didn`t sis! You`ve saved me for one!"

"But Jack`s out there, part of that…that poisonous charnal house that is no-man`s land! And I loved him, Alfred, I loved him so!"

It was now Alfred`s turn to comfort his sister. He held her as she wept on his shoulder, very near to a small wooden style that led to a field of barley.

*

Although Alfred found it hard to grip with his right hand, he had doggedly taught himself to write with his left hand, so he was pronounced fit for duty the following week. Thankfully, however he was to be posted to Harwich, to a staff position at the Training Centre. During his convalescence he had renewed his postal friendship with Emily, Jack`s cousin in Manchester, and Lydia was thrilled to hear that Alfred had even promised to visit her on his next leave – whenever that might be.

The day they waved Alfred off for Harwich at the station, Henry turned to Lydia and said, "I don`t see any point in you renting that cottage now Lydia. Perhaps you should give some thought to returning to your old job at school."

This was the last thing Lydia wanted to do.

"That`s extremely good of you father, but you see I am hoping to return to France. Although it looks like we have routed the enemy, there is still a great need for nurses…"

She got no further. Her father raised his hand to silence her then walked away. Her mother simply shook her head and said "Oh, Lydia," and followed him.

*

She now visited Edwin most days. His face lit up when he saw her, and his eyes would fill with tears when she left. Alfred had warned her that he was becoming too reliant on her, and she knew that only too well.

"You may find it hard to believe, but I have become extremely fond of him. I know a lot of our relationship is built on my compassion for him – I refuse to call it pity. Besides he's teaching me to play chess."

Lydia and Alfred had been deeply moved by Sassoon's war poems, and she understood that he had articulated the reality for a lot of men who had lived through it but could never talk about it.

"It's the truth Lydia, in his powerful, sensitive way he is expressing all the horror and insanity of this…this madness. I never thought I'd be grateful to a bloody poet! Always been a bit of a Philistine where the arts are concerned," Edwin told her. "One line sums war up for me;"

The hell where youth and laughter go.

*

He now spent most of his time in his bath chair – walking exhausted him too much; his prosthetic leg was too painful. But just as in the Home, she enjoyed their times together. She was able to draw out the softer, more tolerant side of his nature. To her amazement he could play a little on the piano, and she encouraged him to practise.

201

One day in the library she gazed around at the huge collection of books.

"Oh, Edwin, you have such a wealth of knowledge in here. I would never get tired of looking and reading."

"Then do just that," he said.

"What?"

"Stay here with me. Enjoy the books to your heart's content. Help me to see what you can see."

Lydia blinked. "But I can`t Edwin. I came to tell you, I`m going back to France shortly."

He stared at her; his face gradually clouding in anger. "But you can`t … you…you…" He coughed until she thought he would choke. She gave him water, and gradually his breathing returned to normal.

"I`m sorry Edwin, I didn`t mean to upset you, but you have a nurse …"

"I don`t want you to be my bloody nurse! I love you Lydia. I've always loved you, even that day in the lane – what a bloody arrogant swine I was – even then I loved you. I`m asking you to marry me."

Lydia was too overwhelmed to reply, and Edwin was now gasping for air and sobbing. "I really am only half a man, I could never love you properly," he paused to cough, "can`t be any damned good to you at all. Except I can give you all all this – for a while. You wouldn`t have to put up with me for long."

"Oh, Edwin, if I married you, it would be for you, nothing else."

"I know I don`t deserve you. Oh God, if this hadn`t happened – oh, I would have been the proudest man in England to walk you down the aisle!

What a pair we would have made! I have dreamt about it, many times; me whole and virile again; the lovely Lydia by my side."

Her heart went out to him – he was feverish but she couldn't believe what she was hearing. She too had similar dreams, only it had been her and Jack walking down the aisle.

"I know you never wanted me," he said as if he read her thoughts, "but if you marry me you can make my dream come true, and I can give you some security in return. We both know it won't be for a lifetime."

All Lydia could say was "Oh Edwin," and she knelt beside him and took him in her arms.

Lydia tossed and turned that night, wondering what to do. She had become deeply fond of Edwin, and she knew that he probably wouldn't live for long, and she could make his final days happy ones. But Jack, her darling Jack. She simply couldn't extinguish that tiny flame of hope, that vision within her, that he was alive somewhere. Miracles happened didn't they? Not only in the bible, but she herself had witnessed the survival of hopeless cases in the wards. She had heard of the rare occasions when men thought to be dead had stumbled back into the trenches. Soldiers with amnesia had turned up months later. She couldn't commit herself to Edwin without making further enquiries. His father was dead, but what about his mother? If anyone would know the unadulterated truth it would be his mother. Could she? Dare she? Could she dare to intrude on a mother's privacy and grief? A woman, a mother, for whom Jack had shown little fondness. What would she make of a little nobody like her turning up on her doorstep? Well, she couldn't do that, but perhaps she could enquire at the family law practice, Albright, Fanshaw and ... somebody. Yes, she would go to Leamington Spa and enquire at the Family Firm. Surely they could tell her something, anything?

Twenty Four

Albright, Fanshaw and Stafford was easy to find in Warwick Street, and from the moment she crossed the imposing portals, Lydia felt she was entering a Dickens' novel. After waiting for over an hour, meeting the formidable Josiah Fanshaw, in his Victorian tail-coat, high collar and shock of white hair, did nothing to dispel this feeling.

Seated as if on a throne in his high-backed leather chair behind an immense mahogany desk, he surveyed Lydia through a curtain of white eyebrows. She felt small and insignificant facing him seated on a small plain chair. He took a file from a pile at his side, and sifted through a few papers. His voice was surprisingly deep and sonorous.

"Ah yes. As I thought. Your, ahem, small allowance? I confirm it was terminated by The Right Honourable Francis Albright…"

Lydia interrupted him. "I know that of course. I am not here about that allowance."

His eyebrows shot up alarmingly.

"Jack Albright was a very dear friend of mine. In fact we were engaged to be married, that is why he arranged for the allowance…" Lydia coughed and hesitated. The oak panelled walls seemed to be closing in on her; her voice sounded so light and feeble in this oppressive atmosphere. She stood up.

"I'm not here for money. I was told he was posted missing after one of the later battles on the Somme. I thought that perhaps you might have more information…I need to know if there is hope…"

"Please do not distress yourself Miss Winters. I'm afraid you have come to the wrong place for that information."

"Then please tell me where Mrs. Albright lives. I must see Jack's mother."

"Once again, that is information that I am not at liberty to disclose. Now, if that will be all?"

"Yes that will be all." Lydia felt on the verge of tears, but she drew herself to her full height and left the office with her head held high.

Back on the street she paused to take a deep breath. No wonder Jack dreaded the thought of ever working there. Well, it had been a mistake to humiliate herself by this visit, and she might walk round endlessly trying to find Jack's home. But she had to try. She had wanted to avoid that, but now that she was here, she would. At the very least she could ask people in the street. As she began walking she heard someone call her name. She looked round to find a tall, hawk-nosed woman in spectacles hurrying to catch up with her.

"I know I shouldn't be doing this, but here. Mrs. Albright's address." She thrust a piece of paper at Lydia, glancing nervously back to the solicitor's premises.

"Why, thank you. Thank you very much."

The woman pulled down her costume jacket, and collected herself. "Jack – Mr. Albright – worked here for a short while before the war. Everyone liked him, even though it was obvious he had no interest in the law – if I may be permitted to say so. I really am so very sorry that no-one can be sure... I mean, it must be dreadful for you."

Lydia smiled graciously. It must have taken a great deal of courage for this woman to have risked her job. She must have been listening to her interview with Mr. Fanshaw, and obviously risked dismissal.

"He was so charming." The woman blinked furiously behind her glasses. "Even to an old stick like me. He gave me a rose you know. I pressed it. No-one has ever given me anything like that. I do hope he will come back." And then she turned abruptly and strode off back to her office, her head held high.

So that was Miss Harcourt! Lydia smiled as she remembered Jack`s letters to her at the time, describing the utter boredom of his time at the office. He had told her about failing to melt old Hardboard`s heart by giving her a rose. Little did he know!

*

Lydia took tea at the Pump Rooms to gather her strength before her task in hand. Eventually she set out for Leam Terrace and lifted the huge, brass knocker on the door of the address Miss Harcourt had given her.

It took a long time before the maid answered the door, and when Lydia told her who she was, and that she wished to see Mrs. Albright, she grinned a wide toothless smile, stood back for her to enter, then retreated to inform her mistress.

"Tell her to get out! Out, out, you imbecile!"
Lydia heard her screamed response in the hallway, and she pushed past the maid. Oh, no, she had come this far; it was now or never.

The room was in semi-darkness.

"How dare you! Get Out! Get Out! Tilly, fetch Watling!"

As Lydia`s eyes adjusted to the gloom she could see a tall, stately figure dressed in a beautiful old fashioned dark green gown, many pearls garlanded round her neck. The formidable Esther Albright.

"But ma`am, Watling left us last year," Tilly protested.

"Then fetch the police, we have an intruder!"

"Give me ten minutes, I am not going to harm your mistress, I beg you," Lydia said to Tilly, who nodded, wide-eyed with excitement. She left the room, but remained listening at the slightly open door.

"Please, Mrs. Albright, I know this is terribly rude, but I must speak to you, for me it is a matter of life and death." Lydia implored.

"Rude? It is positively criminal! You are trespassing, and the police shall throw you out on the street where you belong! I would expect no better behaviour from an ignorant little school teacher – or are you a nurse now? Making your way down the social ladder, God knows where you are now! In the gutter, I hope where you deserve to be!"

This tirade made Lydia tremble. She felt nauseous as she held on to the back of a chair in front of her. "Why do you hate me so? This is the first time you`ve laid eyes on me!"

"Yes, and you`re just as I imagined you to be." Esther Albright walked towards her, and Lydia felt glad the chair was between them. Even in the bad light she could see Esther`s face, so twisted in hate that she looked ugly. How could this be Jack's mother?

"Yes, a pretty face, but then all men fall for a pretty face. But no class, no bearing. Whatever made you think you would ever be accepted into this family?"

"I see now that would have been impossible. All I wanted..." Lydia found it hard to find the words, the woman terrified her so. "All I want..."

"Want! Want! I might have guessed you would want something. I know all about you!" she thrust a finger into Lydia's chest - "how you inveigled your way into my niece's affections. And very nicely you've done by it too! And you want! You want more do you? Well it's a good job I got wind of that allowance when my husband died and I soon put a stop to that!"

"I was so sorry to hear of your husband's death Mrs. Albright." Lydia mumbled.

"Sorry. Mmm. Well I wasn't sorry. He was a man of straw! A weak philanderer." Esther's voice dropped so that her voice was only just audible. She walked back and sat in her chair. "Oh, I didn't care about his women, it meant he left me alone. But as a member of parliament he had the chance to be someone, to make his mark. Most men in his position have been knighted after his years of service. I should have been Lady Albright! All his talk of 'sitting in the house', being away at London. Sitting in his club and spending time with his whores more like! And all on my father's money! Oh, he was landed gentry alright, but penniless. Because my family's money came from business – trade his family called it, they thought we were their social inferiors! But it was my money, MINE! I made Francis Albright, and look how he thanked me! What a fool I was."

Lydia listened to the ticking of a clock as no words were spoken for many minutes. Lydia hardly dared breath in the oppressive air. She had never dreamt that even in Jack`s family this class difference issue simmered and festered causing such bitterness. Esther seemed to have forgotten that she was there as she stared into a fire screen on which a mediaeval knight knelt before a beautiful damsel. She thought of Lancelot, of Jack. When she did eventually speak again, it made Lydia jump.

"SO you see how important it is to make a good marriage, ha!" She stood up. She was smiling as she walked towards Lydia once more. "But not to my Jack!" she spat out at her.

"Just tell me Mrs. Albright, I have to know! Have you heard anything since... is Jack alive?"

Lydia could see her eyes narrow, and glint as she snarled "Jack is dead, you imbecile! Now get out!"

Suddenly Lydia came to life. She wanted to strike out at this bitter harridan. Instead she dashed towards the far end of the room and grabbed one of the heavy red velvet drapes at the window and pushed them aside. As dust billowed out, she pushed the other side, and the bright sunlight of a June afternoon flooded the room. She turned round and almost expected the woman to crumble to dust, and would not have been surprised to see rich cobwebs draped around the place like in Miss Havisham`s room, but she saw that it was a richly furnished well-kept room. Esther Albright covered her face and screamed again and again for her to get out. Tilly was now in the doorway, beckoning anxiously to Lydia.

"Oh, I'm going Mrs. Albright, but if what you say is true, why are you not wearing mourning? You lost your husband and son within months of each other, and you sit here as if you are about to be whisked off to a ball!"

"Oh, I've mourned. I've mourned for years! Jack was never going to amount to anything – feckless like his father. But Thomas, Thomas may take the cloth you know. One day he may be a bishop." Esther Albright now affected a sing-song tone. Shielding her eyes she walked towards a side table and picked up a fan and fanned herself. She was wearing some kind of white make-up and rouge, which had gathered in rivulets along the lines of her face. "And my darling daughter. She will of course be presented at Court. I will have to start preparing for the season. Now, if you'll excuse me..."

By now Lydia realised that Esther Albright was not quite right in the head. She regarded her with pity as she watched her settle back down into her chair and close her eyes. She had always been a hard, emotionless woman, Jack had told her that much, but the events of the past four years had taken its toll on even her indomitable strength.

Tilly came in and drew the curtains closed again, then led Lydia to the door.

"Why do you stay here, Tilly?" Lydia asked.

"Now, where would I go at my age? Me and the old lady, well we'm stuck with each other, en't we? It's 'ardly surprising' that she's off her rocker.

Master Thomas away at war now, and young Theresa at school, her `usband and son dead ... ooh, I`m sorry Miss, but I`ll never forget the day she got the telegram. She read it quick and threw it in the fire. `Master Jack`s dead Tilly.` Just that, and I`ve never heard his name mentioned again – until today."

As Lydia made her way back to the station she wondered why she had not simply asked Tilly what she needed confirming instead of putting herself through that awful confrontation. After all servants knew as much, if not more than their masters and mistresses, she mused, thinking of Polly. But no, she would always have thought that Jack had been exaggerating when he had talked of his mother. Poor Jack, no wonder he valued Alfred`s friendship so, and our family life, such as it was.

For the umpteenth time she imagined taking Jack in her arms and promising to love and cherish him forever. But now she knew that it could not be; her vision would have to remain like her poems, something to comfort and cherish, but never to become reality.

She recalled Wordsworth;

"To grieve not, but rather find, strength in what remains behind."

Twenty Five

Lydia and Edwin were married quietly in Claines Church one early morning in July. Alfred got compassionate leave to be Edwin's best man. Lydia dressed in a light linen suit and carried a small bouquet of pink roses that her mother had made for her. She thought of the pressed buttercups she kept still with the letters in her rosewood box.

Henry walked her down the aisle and gave his daughter away.

"I suppose it's a better option than France," he had said when she told him of her intention to marry. She knew she was destined never to please him.

"Will this make you happy, Lyddy?" Alfred asked her.

"Happy? I don't ever expect to be really happy again Alfred, but I do feel a kind of love for him. Most important of all I know he loves me and needs me, and by doing this, I can make HIM happy." She turned her head away, and added quietly, "for as long as he has."

"And what then?" Alfred's voice took on a harsher tone. "Who will you look after then? First the hospitals, then the convalescent home, then me, now Edwin ... is this going to be your life Lydia, sacrificing yourself over and over again?"

"Sacrificing myself? Oh, Alfred, don't be so melodramatic! I am a nurse, it is what nurses do, what I always wanted to do. Hundreds, thousands of women have become nurses during this abominable war. For many it was simply an extension of what they did before, and for those who sought adventure or escape from their humdrum pampered lives. Once

213

over the shock of reality, they found they could actually be of use, that there was a point to their existence after all. And what will we do when it's all over? You're right, Alfie. We won't be needed in the same way anymore, but things are changing. Women have shown they can do men's jobs, in the fields, the factories. Women over thirty have got the vote. Women like Ada and the Suffragettes have led the way, and perhaps even the lowliest, poorest skivvy will one day realise that she has a choice."

"A choice?" Alfred sounded incredulous.

"Yes, other than to get married and bear children, and work her fingers to the bone; to be at the beck and call of her husband and have no rights whatsoever."

"I fear that may take some time. Things will revert to the status quo after the war, the men will return to their jobs – if they're still there, and women will do what they have always done, look after the children and what's left of the men."

"Yes, women will always be the ones who nurture, but for some of us it's also been a journey of self-discovery. All I wanted was to be Jack's wife, I loved him so, but destiny had other ideas. Ada and the wonderful women like her have shown me that there are other paths to walk, causes to work for."

"And what will your cause be?"

"Who knows? One thing at a time, dear brother. I'll be walking down the aisle tomorrow, and I'll be a happy bride Alfie, I promise. How can I not be, when Edwin looks at me with such love and adoration?"

On their wedding night, they lay together, Edwin stroking her hair crying silent tears for the man he used to be, and Lydia kissed away his tears with words of love and affection.

"I can`t believe you`re here, lying next to me." He whispered.

"I`ll always be here," she soothed.

And she was. On fine days they would take the air, and she often drove the Vauxhall (the Bugatti had been sold long ago) to riverside beauty spots for picnics, and when housebound she would read from Sir Walter Scott`s Waverley novels, or they would play endless games of chess. She sought out appropriate sheet music, and they spent many a happy hour, Lydia singing and Edwin accompanying her on the piano. She invited their few friends to lunch or dinner, the occasions often ending with a sing-song. Sir Frederick and Lady Amelia frequently commented on how joy and laughter had once more entered the Grange.

At last the church bells rang in Claines church as they did all over England on November 11th, Armistice Day. The bloody conflict was over at last, Germany defeated. There were celebrations – Lydia went to the school and helped with the party for the children – and gradually the men who had survived began drifting home. Many were home for Christmas, including Alfred, and Lydia entertained her family to a grand Christmas Lunch at the Grange. Edwin had never completely mastered his prosthetic leg, but he had worn it to walk Lydia down the aisle and strapped it on to ride a little, and he wore it Christmas day to stand and welcome his guests, who

215

included some younger cousins and friends of his younger sister home from boarding school. The house was filled with light, laughter and music, just as Lydia had hoped it would be, when she had worked hard to decorate and plan the meals. And she was able to laugh along with the rest of them, but always there was an empty void in her heart that nothing could fill.

In the middle of January Edwin took a turn for the worst. An influenza epidemic was sweeping the country; first a chambermaid became ill, then ironically Edwin's nurse. Edwin succumbed and died within two days, with Lydia, as always, at his side.

"We shall be selling The Grange now," Sir Frederick informed Lydia shortly after the funeral. This came as no surprise to her, as Sir Frederick had been gradually selling off parts of the estate during the past two years.

"Frankly my dear we have more debts than assets. Harriet wants us to go and live with her in India, but Lady Amelia couldn't stand the heat. Her brother – you met the family at Christmas of course – has a fine estate near Shrewsbury, and the Dower House is simply begging to be taken over and made something of. It'll be nice for Margaret to have her cousins to play with, and Lady Amelia to have her family ..."

Lydia felt sorry for the proud old Squire, who was obviously putting a brave face on things, and was probably dreading the move, having to rely on the generosity of his in-laws.

"I'm afraid I also have to inform you that there is little for you to inherit as Edwin's widow. There is the library of course, and his trust which he inherited at twenty one. Unfortunately, much of that was eaten up with the cost of his convalescence, but there will be something… enough I hope, dear Lydia, to sustain you for a while. Of course nothing can repay you for your love and devotion to our son …"

"Oh, Sir Frederick, (Lydia had never been able to call him 'father' as he had requested many times). I loved Edwin and I would never have changed the last six months for anything. Please believe that."

He told her to stay as long as she wanted, so Lydia remained for a few weeks to help oversee the heart-breaking task of making inventories of the furniture and fittings which were to be sold, as neither Sir Frederick or Lady Amelia could face it.

Alfred visited her one day, and waited as she was showing round a prospective buyer.

"You do amaze me little sister. You have faultlessly evolved into Lady of the Manor. Shame it was never to be. Are you sorry you won't be staying on?"

"No, but I have to help Sir Frederick, he's such a broken man now. Can you believe this place is the same house we came to for that Summer Ball nearly four years ago?" Lydia gestured towards the walls now stripped of the golden framed paintings, the few remaining pieces of furniture stripped of the china and expensive ornaments. Even the massive chandeliers looked dusty and forlorn. She took Alfred's arm and led him to the basement kitchen.

"Have to make my own tea now, as there is only cook and one other of other servant left now."

"My God, how on earth do you manage?" Alfred teased.

As she put the kettle on the hob and assembled cups and saucers, Lydia told Alfred that Sylvia had written to her from London.

"She's now Matron of a Home in the East End, run by one of Ada's charities which supports widows and orphans. Naturally since the war there are so many more, and help is desperately needed."

"Oh, no!" Alfred groaned. "So now you're going to slave away for the widows and orphans."

"Yes, and why not?" Lydia bridled. "I learnt a lot from Ada about lobbying and fund raising. I won't be scrubbing floors and wiping noses necessarily."

"That's a relief then"

Lydia grinned and poured the boiling water into the tea pot, just as the kitchen door was flung open and Sarah Ganderton almost fell into the kitchen.

"Thank God you'm 'ere Master Alfred," she gasped. "Come quick, Master's collapsed!"

Twenty Six

A week later a young stranger paused at the gateway to the Mug Inn. He stood aside to allow a couple dressed in mourning to pass. The man doffed his cap at the stranger who had the unmistakeable bearing of a gentleman. The gentleman nodded in acknowledgement, thinking there was something familiar about the man. It could be the village blacksmith, he thought, but if it was, he had aged considerably.

He looked towards the graveyard and noticed the fresh mound of earth with two flowered wreaths on the rise to his right and shivered. He stepped inside the warm fug of the Inn, and could see very little had changed. Wally Trump was still behind the bar, and he noticed that the other customers were also dressed in black. The air was thick with pipe and tobacco smoke.

"A funeral then?" the young man said, stating the obvious, as Wally poured his brandy.

"Ar. Village Schoolmaster. Big turnout."

"Mr. Winters?"

"Ar, that's right." Wally looked at the stranger closely. "You'm not from round yer, but I seems to know y'face if yer don't mind me sayin' Sir."

"I did spend some time here in the summer of 1914. Before ..." He gulped the brandy.

"Ar, Sir. I know, seems a lifetime ago. Saw some action then?"

"Some." He nodded at the glass, and Wally obligingly re-filled it. The young man needed another drink before he could ask the next question, but Wally second guessed him.

"Captain Winters made it through like you, but p`raps you already knows that, Sir."

Some of the tension left the stranger`s face. "No, no I didn`t know ... Splendid!"

"Another Sir?"

He nodded. "Alfred`s sister...Lydia. How is Lydia?" He gripped the glass tightly. Please God ...

"Oh Lady Lydia`s done alright for `erself, considerin` her buried her father today..."

"Lady Lydia?" The young man gasped.

The look on the gentleman`s face took Wally aback. "Well, not strickly speakin`, but her did marry the squire`s son, even though..."

"Wally! Let`s get some service yer!"

Wally was cut off by the raucous demand of one of the locals a little worse for wear, banging his tankard on the bar.

"Alright, alright!" Wally looked at the young gentleman. "You don`t look well Sir. I`d sit down if I was you."

The stranger loosened the top buttons on his great coat and gulped down the brandy. He needed air. He almost fell into a couple sitting near the door, as he stumbled outside. Had he been able to focus, he would have recognised Polly and Freddie.

"Polly! You knows who that was don`t yer?" hissed Freddie.

"Yes. It was Master Jack back from the dead. Well I never." Polly lifted her glass of port calmly to her lips.

"Well, you `eard what Wally told `im, or rather what he didn`t tell `im. Master Jack looked shocked to the core. `e thinks as Lydia`s lady of the manor.

Wally didn't get round to telling' 'im as Edwin's dead."

"So what? "

"For pity's sake Polly, you could see as he was shattered, and God knows what he's been through already. I bet he's come back for Lydia."

"Huh! Lucky Lydia, or perhaps not."

"I don't understand why you dislikes her so."

"Oh don't yer? P'raps its 'cos you likes her so, and because hers so bloody self-satisfied with all her do-goodin. I'll never forgive her interferin' when Aggie killed yer dad. We was landed with 'er good and proper, thanks to Lady Lydia."

"You can be so spiteful Polly, d'ye know that? Well I'm goin' after 'im and I'm goin' to tell him Lydia's free and up at School House, right now!"

"You do Freddie Maycroft, and you'll find the door locked when you gets 'ome. Besides, you'll never catch him up."

Freddie knew she was right, but he limped outside anyway. He went as far as the kissing gate and looked down the lane. There was no-one to be seen. He hoped that Master Jack had gone to School House to see Master Alfred, and he would tell him. Better still he'd see Lydia himself. He made his way back to the Inn, and as he did so, he could make out some-one standing by Mr. Winters' grave.

Jack had seen enough graves and headstones to last him into eternity, but all the same he staggered towards the newly dug grave. Ha! He might as well lie down next to Lydia's father, for the very thing that had kept him alive the past two years was now lost to him.

He may just as well have been buried alive after all, after a bullet had felled him in No-Man's Land during the battle for the Transloy Ridges. But he had been picked up off the battlefield by the Germans a day later. The Red Cross had missed him as he had been half buried by mud and German bodies. One of the Hun stretcher bearers had pilfered his identification bracelet – which like many other officers he had commissioned to be made in silver – so no-one had ever been notified of his status as a prisoner of war. The bullet had just missed his brain, and a skilled German surgeon had removed it, but he had suffered amnesia for most of his incarceration. He had managed to escape with another fellow officer when they were being transferred by train to another camp. They had been sheltered by a French farming family for a couple of months, near Cambrai.

By then, snatches of the past had begun to form in his mind, many initiated by Percy, his fellow escapee. He would often whistle tunes that brought back memories of school and university. Percy had been at Cambridge, but their backgrounds had obviously been similar, as Percy's recollections began to stimulate his own.

They would toil in the fields for the farmer in return for the meagre rations they were able to share with them, and the farmer's daughter, Gabrielle would work alongside. Jack smiled at her memory. She was barely fifteen, but behind her father's back she would try to steal kisses from the boys. On one occasion, sheltering from the rain in the barn, she surprised Jack, making it obvious that she wanted more than kisses, and Jack had been tempted. He took her in his arms and kissed her properly for the first time, and at the touch of her lips and the warmth of her body, the memory of Lydia overwhelmed him. He pushed away this pale imitation of his true love and ran and knelt in the stubbled field, laughing with joy as image after image of his time with Lydia flooded his mind as the rain drenched his face.

He was feverish for days afterwards; poor little Gabrielle nursing him with cold compresses and hot soup. Yes, one day he would go back to Cambrai and thank Gabrielle and her family.

There had been a battle nearby – one of the last of the war - and he and Percy had joined up with a Canadian Unit – had even helped take a machinegun post. The rest had been a blur – being transferred back to a British battalion; lots of confusion and red tape and finally being shipped back across the channel and formally discharged. Meeting up with the remnants of his old regiment filled in more gaps of his history.

Lydia burned bright in his mind, but he lacked the courage to return, feeling a shadow of his former self. He knew his home was in Leamington, but his whole being recoiled against it, despite the fact that his childhood memories were few. He merely wrote to say he was alive and well.

He had enough back pay to fund a trip to the lakes, this time staying in a humble little fell cottage. He walked and walked, reliving his holiday with Alfred, filling in more gaps in his memory. All the time he was gaining in strength, building up the confidence to go and find Lydia.

He bent down and looked at the wreath of white roses.

"Rest in Peace dear Father, Your loving daughter Lydia."

The tears that had been threatening to overwhelm him ran unchecked down his cheeks. Just a short while ago she had touched these flowers; these were her words, he knew the writing so well. He remembered a poem and a pressed buttercup, lost long ago. Lydia – now lost to him too. No point in visiting the family now. He would have loved to see his old friend and comrade, Alfred, but he couldn't bear to see Lydia on the arm of another man.

*

Freddie watched as Jack knelt weeping at the graveside, then returned to his wife in the Inn.

"Back are yer, then? Come on, I've got you another drink. Get it down yer, yer looks perished."

"He`s at the grave Polly, cryin` his eyes out."

"Didn`t know he thought that much of Mr. Winters."

"He `en`t grieving` for Mr. Winters, and you know it."

"Oh, for `eaven`s sake! I`m off `ome. You do what you like!"

Polly pulled on her best black coat and straightened her hat. She glanced up at the grave as she left the Inn, and saw Master Jack kneeling at the graveside.

He`ll catch his death, she thought, silly bugger. As she reached the kissing gate Lydia came walking down the hill. Well, would you believe it? She felt sick.

"Not stayin' with yer mam tonight then?" she managed to say as she drew level.

"No Polly. Alfred's there, and a cousin from mother's family who came to the funeral. I'm going into Barbourne to stay with Lizzie." She noticed Polly's odd demeanour. "Are you alright Polly?"

"Y…yes, I'm fine. Had one port too many I think. Well, I'll bid you good day, Lydia."

"Thank you for coming today Polly." Lydia reached out and touched Polly's hand that was gripping the gate post. "Dear Polly."

Polly swallowed hard and turned away, as Lydia carried on walking. Dear Polly! Dear Polly am I? She began to hyperventilate and she held onto the gate post for dear life, fighting back the tears.

"Are you alright madam?"

Through the blur of tears she made out Master Jack. A man now, sure enough with his moustache and homburg hat, and there were flecks of grey in his black hair showing beneath. But there was no mistaking those dark eyes. Dancin', twinkling' eyes they used to be, now all red from cryin'.

"Ar, I'm alright. Think I 'ad a bit of a turn. Just getting' me breath back."

"I know you! My goodness, Polly! How lovely to see you again."

Oh, still the charmer! "And you Master Jack. Look at you! Mud all over yer coat and trousers. You'll be askin' me to clean 'em up for you next thing you know."

"Oh, Polly! Would that you could. Would that we could go back to that summer, eh?"

225

Polly watched Lydia disappearing into the distance.

"Well you `ave come back. Come back for Lydia `ave you?"

"I know I`m too late Polly" he choked.

Polly grasped his arm. "No! She did marry Edwin Bengeworth, married `im out of pity. He was gassed and crippled in the war, but he died. She`s a widow Jack!"

Jack looked at her in confusion.

"She`s walkin` down the lane Jack look!"

She stood aside so that he could pass through the gate. He ran into the road and looked down the lane. He could just make out a small dark figure in the distance.

"Yes, it`s her, it`s Lydia. Well, you come back for `er didn`t yer? Well go and bloody get `er!"

When Lydia had left Polly she mused that her old friend had looked very pale, but in spite of their estrangement when she had reached for her hand, she had detected a spark of the old affection that she knew had once been there. Ah, well, nothing surprised her any more.

It had been a time of great sorrow for the family, most of all for her mother of course. Her relationship with her father had always been strained, but she had been glad that his attitude had softened since her marriage to Edwin, and she had happy memories of Henry enjoying the last Christmas and other times with the Squire and his family at the Grange, and he had been loving and kind to her after Edwin`s death.

Her decision to return to London would have to wait. Her mother would need her for a while.

She reached the style to the barley field and paused, as she always did. It was obscured now with the gathering mist, but she knew that it was muddy and bare. She shivered, closed her eyes and for the millionth time, relived that moment four years ago, when against the swaying barley and the setting sun, Jack had looked into her eyes and the world had tipped on its axis. Oh Jack!

"Lydia!"

He was calling to her, as in her dreams. He had called to her many, many times from the mud of France.

"Lydia, oh Lydia."

He sounded so real. She opened her eyes. It wasn't a dream, he was here! No! Who was this wild eyed man, gasping for breath? She took a step back. Then he smiled a crooked smile, and his eyes softened. She knew those eyes.

He took off his hat and held it to his chest. His hair was flecked with grey, oh, no, my lovely young Jack's curly hair. She reached out and touched it gently. He dropped his hat and stood there, still struggling to regain his breath, as tears streaked his face and mingled with the sweat from running. She stepped forward and wiped away his tears, and felt the deep scar at the side of his forehead.

War, The Hell Where Youth and laughter go.

"What happened?"
"Shot, left for dead. A long story."

"All this time …but it is you, my lovely, brave knight. You`ve come back to me. Hold me Jack. Don`t disappear like in my dreams."

"Never. We`ll never be parted again. No-one, nothing can come between us ever again. Always and forever, my darling."

The two young lovers held each other tight for a very long time. Lydia and Jack; destined to be together against all the odds, since that moment nearly five years before when the look of love had passed between them in a summer field of barley.

THE END

9548942R00129

Printed in Great Britain
by Amazon.co.uk, Ltd.,
Marston Gate.